Fr

SOPHENE

Published by Sophene 2019

Armenian Tales was first published in 2019 by Sophene Pty Ltd.

These tales were originally translated to the English language by A.G. Seklemian and Z. C. Boyajian.

www.sophenebooks.com
www.sophenearmenianlibrary.com

ISBN-13: 978-1-9259-3707-7

ARMENIAN TALES

A COLLECTION OF CLASSIC ARMENIAN FOLK TALES

ARMENIAN TALES

A COLLECTION OF CLASSIC ARMENIAN FOLK TALES

CONTENTS

THE FOOL

Once upon a time there was a man who inherited much wealth from his father, but who led such an irregular and unwise life that in a short time he had spent everything, even down to the last penny. Then he sat down, folded his arms upon his chest, and sighed as he thought of his unfortunate condition. His father's friends gathered about him to console him. One of them, a wise old man, said to him:

"Son, you have offended your Luck, who has run away from you. You would better go after your Luck; perchance you can find it, and being reconciled with it become, as before, a fortunate man."

The man at once set out and travelled mountains and plains in search of his Luck. One night he saw in his dreams that his Luck was a human being like himself, who had fallen upon his face on the top of a high mountain, sighing and beating his chest all the time, just as he himself had done. The next day, he got up and continued his journey toward that mountain. On his way he met the Fairy Lion, sitting upon a mound of earth beside the road.

"Don't be afraid, human being, proceed," said the Lion. And when the man approached, he said: "Where are you going?"

"I am going to find my Luck," said the man.

"Good!" said the Lion, "your Luck is very wise; ask him what is the remedy for my disease. I have been an invalid for seven years. If you find the right remedy I will reward you."

"Very well," said the man, and went on his way. Soon he came to a very beautiful orchard full of all kinds of fruits. He picked some of the fruits and began to eat, but lo! They were all bitter. Thereupon the gardener came and asked where he was going.

"I am going to find my Luck," said the man.

"Please ask your Luck," said the gardener, "what is the remedy for my orchard. I grafted my plants, but it was of no use. I cut down the old trees and planted new ones, but neither did this avail. If your Luck can devise some remedy, I will reward you bountifully." The man promised to ask his Luck, and again went on his way. Soon he came to a magnificent palace situated in a garden as beautiful as paradise, whose sole inhabitant was a beautiful maiden.

"What man are you?" asked the maiden, seeing the man, "and why have you come?"

The man told her his story.

"You see," said the maiden, "I have this splendid palace and measureless wealth and property; but I have a grief which grows in my heart day and night, and I spend my life sighing all the time. Please ask your Luck about me, and if you bring me a device to make me happy, I promise to reward you bountifully."

The man promised, and went on his way until he came to the mountaintop where his Luck had fallen on his face. He described to him his own unfortunate condition, and poured out all his grievances. Luck listened to him attentively, and said:

"Everything may yet be well, seeing that you have come so far in search of me."

Then the man asked of Luck the things he had promised to ask, and received answers.

"Now will you not come with me?" asked the man.

"Go first," said Luck, "I will come after you."

The man set out, and, coming first to the young woman,

said, “Your remedy is to marry a brave fellow, and then your sorrow and grief will be over.”

Then he met the gardener, and said:

“There is gold-ore in the spring from which flows the water with which you irrigate your orchard. The plants suck up particles of gold, which causes the fruits to be bitter. You must either irrigate your orchard by the water of some other spring, or take away the ore from the present fountain—then your fruits will be sweet.”

The man then came to the lion and sat down beside him, and told him how he found his Luck, and all about the vineyard-owner, and about the young woman. The lion asked, “Didn’t the young woman do you any kindness?”

The man replied, “She said, ‘Come and marry me, and let us enjoy together the goodness of God.’ But I did not consent.”

“And what reward did the gardener give you?” asked the Lion.

“He took the gold ore out of the spring,” answered the man, “along with a great deal of pure gold. He offered that I take everything, but I declined, saying that I did not care to trouble myself and carry such a heavy thing so far.”

“And what remedy did your Luck devise for my ailment?” asked the Lion.

“And for you, he said ‘the moment you devour a fool’s head you shall be healed.’”

The Lion looked the man in the face, and said:

“By Heaven! I cannot find a greater fool than you on the face of the earth.” And striking at his head with his paw, he made one mouthful of it and the fool was dead.

Remember the moral of this tale—

Time never befriends a fool.

THE OLD WOMAN AND THE CAT

Once upon a time there was an old woman who had a goat. She milked the goat every day and kept the milk in the cupboard; but a sly cat came and licked it up. One day, however, the old woman succeeded in getting hold of the cat, cut off her tail as a punishment, and let her go.

"Meow! meow!" cried the cat; "Give me my tail!"

"Bring me my milk and I will give you your tail," said the old woman.

The cat went to the goat and said: "Goat, kind goat, do give me some milk! I will give it to the old woman and get back my tail."

"Bring me some boughs from that tree, and I will give you milk," answered the goat.

The cat went to the tree and said, "O good tree, do give me some boughs! I will take them to the goat, get a little milk and give it to the old woman, and get back my tail."

"Bring me some water and I will give you some boughs," answered the tree.

The cat went to the water-carrier and said, "Kind water-carrier, give me some water! I will take it to the tree and get some boughs, give them to the goat and get some milk, and give it to the old woman and get my tail."

"Bring me a pair of shoes and I will give you some water," said the water-carrier.

The cat went to the shoemaker and said, "Shoemaker, good shoemaker, do give me a pair of shoes! I will give them to the water-carrier, who will give me some water; I will take it to the tree and get some boughs for the goat; she will give me some milk, which I will take to the old woman and get my tail."

"Bring me an egg and I will give you a pair of shoes," said the shoemaker.

The cat went to the hen and said, "Hen, good hen, do lay me an egg! I will take it to the shoemaker and get a pair of shoes for the water-carrier; he will give me some water, which I will take to the tree and get some boughs for the goat; she will give me some milk, which I will take to the old woman and get my tail."

"Bring me some barley and I will lay an egg for you," answered the hen.

The cat went to the threshing-floor and said, "Threshing-floor, kind threshing-floor, do give me some barley!"

The threshing-floor said: "There, you may gather the scattered barley which my good master has left as food for the birdies and ants."

The cat gathered the barley and took it to the hen, which laid her an egg. She took the egg to the shoemaker and got a pair of shoes. She took the pair of shoes to the water-carrier and got a pailful of water for the tree. The tree gave her some boughs that she took the goat. The goat gave her some milk that she took to the old woman.

"Here is your tail," said the old woman, "and be careful from now on not to steal my milk."

The cat took her tail and tried to stick it in its place but she could not. She tried over and over again to stick it with resin, with tar and with glue, but it was of no use. So that cat has remained tailless to this day, as a sign of her being a thief.

THE FAIRY NIGHTINGALE

A very interesting story was once told me of a King who built a splendid church. It took the architects seven years to finish the building. The King went to dedicate the church and to pray in it, and lo! There was a fog so dense that the King was almost suffocated. In the very midst of the dense fog a monk stood before the King, saying:

"Long live the King! You have built a fine church, but it lacks one thing."

The monk then quickly disappeared. The King came out and ordered his men to take down the building and to put up another one finer than the first. It took them another seven years to finish the second building. The King again went to dedicate the church and pray in it, and lo! Again there was a dense fog, and the same monk stood before the King, saying:

"Long live the King! You have built a beautiful church, but it lacks one thing."

Again the monk mysteriously disappeared. The King again ordered his men to take down the building and to put up a new one. It took them another seven years to finish the third building, and it was this time so splendid that there was nothing like it in the entire world. The King again went to dedicate it and to pray in it, and lo! Again there was a dense fog, and the same monk stood before the King saying:

"Long live the King! You have built a church incomparably beautiful, but it lacks one thing."

The monk was again about to make his exit when the King took hold of his collar, saying:

"Tell me what is the one thing lacking in my church. This is the third time that you compel me to take down my building, upon which so much labor and time have been spent."

"The Fairy Nightingale is the only thing that is lacking in this magnificent church," said the monk, and disappeared in the fog.

The King returned to his palace, and thereafter was very sad. He had three sons, who seeing their father sad, asked:

"Long live the King! What grieves you, father?"

"My sons," said the King, "I am getting old, and the Fairy Nightingale is needed for the church. I do not know how to get it."

"Be of good cheer, father," said the boys, "we will go and bring it."

And they started. After a long journey they came to a place where the road divided into three branches, with a sign on each. The sign of the broad road was—"He who goes on this road returns safely." The sign on the middle road was—"He who goes on this road may return or may not return." And the sign on the third narrow road was—"He who goes on this road never returns." The oldest brother took the broad road; the second brother took the middle road, and the youngest brother took the narrow road. The oldest boy soon came to a large city, at sight of which he said to himself:

"Why should I go farther and be killed? I would better stay in this place." And he became a servant in one of the inns of the city.

The second brother turned toward the other side of the mountain, and came to a green meadow with shady trees here and there, and benches under the trees. He was tired, and at once sat down upon one of the benches. Soon a giant as black as night came along with an iron rod in his hand. He gave the boy one stroke with the rod, and lo! The boy turned into a round stone, and rolled under the bench.

The youngest of the three brothers started on the road along which there could be no return. A dense fog covered him, and lo! The monk who had talked with his father appeared to him, saying:

"Godspeed thee, son! Where are you going?"

"I am going to bring the Fairy Nightingale for our new church," said the boy.

"Good," said the monk; "but this way is dangerous; let me advise you. The owner of the Fairy Nightingale is the Fairy Queen, a very beautiful maiden. On your way you will soon come to a river that the Fairy Queen has by her arts changed into a poisoned stream, and she does not drink of it. But you must drink of it, and say: 'O happy! This is the water of immortality.' After crossing the river you will come to a grove that the queen has changed into a jungle of thorns and thistles. You must smell the trees and shrubs, and say: 'O happy! This grove is the flower of Paradise.' Then you will come to a narrow pass on one side of which there is a wolf bound with chains, and on the other side there is a lamb bound with chains. There is a bundle of grass before the wolf, and a piece of meat before the lamb. You must put the grass before the lamb, and the meat before the wolf. You will then come to a large gate with double doors, one open and one closed. You must open the closed door and shut the open one. Entering in you will find the Fairy Queen, owner of the Fairy Nightingale, sleeping in a splendid bedchamber. She sleeps seven days and nights, and is awake seven days and nights. If you can do what I have told you, and reach there at a time when the Queen is asleep, you can bring the Nightingale; if not, you are lost."

The boy started, and came successively to the river, the grove, the lamb and the wolf, and the gate. He did all that the monk had told him, and entering, saw an exquisite bedchamber where a maiden as beautiful as the sun was sleeping on a purple bed embroidered with gold and jewelry. The Fairy Nightingale came down from its cage, and standing on the Queen's bedside, sang to her a thousand songs with enchanting melody, and lullabied her to sound sleep. The boy, who was watching from behind the arras, seeing the maiden asleep, and that the Nightingale had returned to its cage, crept in slowly, took the Nightingale's cage, pressed a kiss upon the forehead of the sleeping maiden, thus stamping the sign of his lips there, and started back on his way.

The Queen awoke, and seeing the Nightingale had been stolen, exclaimed:

"Doors, catch the thief!"

"Godspeed him!" said the doors; "He closed the open one of us and opened the closed one of us."

"Wolf and lamb, catch the thief!" exclaimed the Fairy Queen.

"Godspeed him!" said the wolf and the lamb; "He gave the meat to the wolf, and the grass to the lamb."

"Grove, catch the thief!" exclaimed the Queen.

"Godspeed him!" said the grove; "You made me thorns and thistles; he made me a flower of Paradise."

"River, catch the thief!" exclaimed the Queen.

"Godspeed him!" said the river; "You made me a stream of poison; he made me the water of immortality."

When the Queen saw that all her charms were unavailing, she mounted her horse and started in pursuit of the boy.

But let us return to the boy. He passed all the dangerous

places and came to the square where the road divided into the three branches. He saw the monk waiting for him.

"Here is the Fairy Nightingale, holy father," said the boy, and seeing that his brothers had not yet come back, gave the cage to the monk and started to search for his brothers. He went first along the broad road, until he came to the inn where his brother was serving. He secretly made himself known to his brother, and brought him to the monk. He then took the next road, and went as far as the green meadow and sat down upon one of the benches. Soon the giant appeared with his iron rod and tried to strike the boy. But the boy cleverly avoided the blow, and snatching the rod from the giant's hand, struck him. Immediately the giant fell down and was changed into a huge round black stone.

"My brother must have been lost somewhere in this place," thought the boy, and began to strike with the iron rod the stones scattered here and there upon the meadow, and lo! The stones were changed into men, who began to run away; but his brother was not among them. He saw a stone under the bench, and struck it. It was changed into his brother, and began to run.

"Brother! Brother, do not run, it is me," exclaimed the boy.

He stopped and both returned to the monk. All three, taking the Fairy Nightingale, went toward their father's city. On the way they were thirsty, and came to a well.

They lowered the youngest brother to get water, and as soon as he reached the bottom of the well, the two older brothers said to one another:

"When we go home to our father all praise and glory will be given to that fellow who is now in the well, and we shall be despised. It shall not be; he shall never come up from that well."

They cut the rope, and leaving the hero in the well, took the Nightingale and went to their father, saying:

"Our youngest brother was killed in our attempt to get the Fairy Nightingale, but we two succeeded in bringing it."

They hung the cage in the new church, but the Fairy Nightingale did not warble a single song; it was sad and silent. Soon the Fairy Queen came riding to the King, and said:

"Who is the hero that has brought my Nightingale?"

"We brought it," said the two brothers.

"Well, what did you meet on the way?" inquired the Queen.

"Nothing," said the boys.

"Then it was not you who brought it," said the Queen; "you are thieves." And she caused them to be arrested and imprisoned, saying:

"You shall not be released until the real hero who brought the Fairy Nightingale is presented to me."

Some women who were gleaning barley in the fields happened to pass near the well where the boy was left, and hearing him groan took him out; one of them, who had no children, adopted him as her son. After a few weeks news came from the city to the village to the effect that the King's sons had brought the Fairy Nightingale, but the Fairy Queen, the owner of the Nightingale, also had come after it. One day the boy asked permission of his adopted mother, saying:

"A new church has been built, let me go and see it."

The old woman consented, and he went to the city as a peasant boy. He went to his father's house and heard that his brothers were imprisoned. He went directly to the prison and set them free. The Fairy Queen, hearing this, came and said to the boy:

"I am the Fairy Queen, the owner of the Nightingale; are you not afraid of me?"

"I am he who brought the Fairy Nightingale," said the boy, "I am not afraid of you."

"What did you see on the way?" asked the Queen.

The boy told her what he had seen and what he had done.

"And moreover," said the boy, "I have put a sign upon your forehead with my own lips. Look at your image in that pond, and you will see that you are my betrothed."

The Queen looked at her reflected image in the water, and seeing the mark of the boy's kiss, exclaimed:

"Hero, you are worthy of me; I am yours hereafter."

A wedding festival for forty days and forty nights was celebrated. After this the couple went to the church to be married. The Fairy Nightingale began to warble, and sang them a thousand and one songs. It is still singing, and the entire world is wondering at its sweet melodies.

Three apples fell from heaven—one for me, one for the story-teller, and one for him who entertained the company.

THE DREAMER

A father and mother once lived whose son was a dreamer. One morning the boy arose and said to his mother:

"Mother, I dreamed a dream last night, but I will not tell it."

"Why will you not tell it?" asked the mother.

"I will not," answered the boy.

The mother beat the boy, who ran to his father, saying:

"Father, I dreamed a dream last night; I did not tell it to mother, and I will not tell it to you."

The father also beat the boy, who was angered and ran away from the house. After a day's journey he met a traveller.

"Good-day!" said the boy.

"Good-day!" replied the traveller.

"I dreamed a dream," said the boy; "I did not tell it to my mother, I did not tell it to my father, and I will not tell it to you."

The boy went on until he came to the Prince's palace. The Prince was sitting at the door. The boy said:

"Prince, I dreamed a dream; I did not tell it to my mother, I did not tell it to my father, I did not tell it to the traveller, and I will not tell it to you."

The Prince was angry, and cast the boy into a prison in the cellar of his palace. The boy dug through the wall of his prison with his dagger and opened a hole into the adjacent room, which happened to be the dining room of the Prince's daughter. The boy, finding the maiden's food in the cupboard, ate it all and withdrew to his prison. Soon the maiden came in, and lo! The food was eaten. This was repeated on several days. The maiden was very anxious to know who it was who ate her food, and one day hiding herself in her wardrobe she began to watch. Soon she saw the boy, who lifting a great stone opened a hole in the wall, crept into her room, took the food from the cupboard and began to help himself. She jumped out, and taking hold of the boy, said:

"Who are you, young man?"

"I dreamed a dream," said the boy, "I did not tell it to my mother, I did not tell it to my father, I did not tell it to the traveller, I did not tell it to the Prince; the Prince cast me into prison, and I dug a hole with my dagger and came here. I am at your mercy."

The maiden fell in love with the boy, and thereafter cherished him not only with her food but also with her love, and they accepted one another as husband and wife.

One day the King of the East sent messengers to the Prince bearing a stick which had both ends equal, saying:

"Now, tell me which is the bottom and which is the top of this stick. If you solve this, well and good; if not, you must give your daughter in marriage to my son."

The Prince called all his wise men into council, but no one could solve the riddle. The princess told it to the boy. The boy said:

"Go and tell your father to tell them to cast the stick into the pond; the bottom end will sink the deeper in the water."

They did so, and the riddle was solved. On the following day the King of the East sent three horses, all being exactly the same size and having the same appearance, saying:

"Which is the one year old colt, which is the two year old colt, and which is the mother? If you solve this, well and good; if not, you must give your daughter in marriage to my son."

All the learned men of the Prince could not solve this riddle. The princess, in the evening, said to the boy:

"No one could solve the riddle, and they will take me away tomorrow."

"Tell your father," said the boy, "to let them keep the horses in the stable over night. In the morning let them take a bundle of hay, wet and salt it and cast it before the horses outside the stable door. The mother will come out first, the two year old colt after her, and the one year old colt last."

They did as the boy advised, and the riddle was solved. On the following day the King of the East sent to the Prince a steel shield and a steel spear, saying:

"If you can pierce this shield with this spear with one stroke, I will give my daughter to your son in marriage; if you cannot pierce it, you must give your daughter to my son in marriage."

The Prince and all his men tried, and could not pierce the shield. The

Prince then said to his daughter:

"Go, send your man; let us see if he can pierce it."

The boy came, and at one stroke pierced the steel shield with the steel spear. Now, the Prince had no son; he therefore adopted the boy, who was already his son-in-law, and made him heir apparent to his throne. Thereupon the boy set out to go and bring the daughter of the King of the East. After a long journey he met a man who was kneeling down with his ear close to the ground.

"What man are you?" asked the boy.

"I lay my ear to the ground," answered the man, "and listen to whatever men say all over the world."

"Aha! What a man!" exclaimed the boy, "He can hear what is said all over the world."

"Man?" said the listener. "A man is he who pierced the steel shield with the steel spear."

"It was me," said the boy.

"Then I am your brother," said the listener, and followed the boy. After another long journey they met a man who was standing with one of his feet upon Mount Ararat and the other upon Mount Taurus.

"Aha! What a man!" exclaimed the boy. "He strides over the world."

"Man?" exclaimed the colossal strider. "A man is he who pierced the steel shield with the steel spear."

"It was me," said the boy.

"Then I am your brother," said the colossus, and followed the boy.

After a long journey they met a man who was eating all the loaves baked in seven ovens, and still crying, "I am hungry! I am starving! For heaven's sake, give me something to eat!"

"Aha!" said the boy. "What a man! whom seven ovens continually baking cannot satisfy."

"Man?" exclaimed the glutton. "A man is he who pierced the steel shield with the steel spear."

"I am the man," said the boy.

"Then I am your brother," said the glutton, and followed the boy.

Soon they met a man who was carrying the earth upon his shoulders.

"What a man!" exclaimed the boy.

"Man?" replied the carrier of the earth. "A man is he who has pierced the steel shield with the steel spear."

"I am the man," said the boy.

"Then I am your brother," said the carrier of the earth, and he also followed the boy.

They soon met a man who was lying flat on the bank of the Euphrates, and drinking the river dry, but still crying, "I am thirsty! I am dry; more water, for heaven's sake!"

"Aha! What a man," exclaimed the boy, "The river Euphrates does not satisfy his thirst."

"Man?" exclaimed the river-drinker, "A man is he who pierced the steel shield."

"I am he," said the boy.

"Then I am your brother," said the river-drinker, and followed the boy.

They soon met a shepherd who was blowing his horn, and lo! Hills and valleys, plains and forests, men and beasts were dancing.

"Aha! What a man!" exclaimed the boy, "All the world is dancing to his music."

"Man!" returned the shepherd, "A man is he who pierced the steel shield."

"I am he," said the boy.

"Then I am your brother," said the shepherd, and he followed the boy. Now they were seven.

"Brother Steel-shield-steel-spear," said the six adopted brothers to the boy, "where shall we go now?"

"We shall go and bring the daughter of the King of the East," answered the boy.

"You are worthy of her," said his six companions.

Soon they arrived at the city of the King of the East, who seeing them said to his servants secretly:

"These seven fellows have come to take away my daughter. Heaven forbid! They are bashful boys and will hardly eat a bowlful of soup. Now go and bake twenty-one ovens full of bread and make twenty-one cauldrons full of soup and put it all before them. If they can eat all at one sitting, I will give them my daughter; if not, I will not."

The boy and his crew were entertained in an apartment some distance from the King's apartment, where he was giving these instructions to his men. The ground-listener, hearing the King's orders, said to the boy:

"Brother Steel-shield-steel-spear, did you hear what the King said to his men?"

"No, nitwit!" said the boy, "How can I hear him while he is in another apartment far from us?"

The ground-listener said: "They are going to serve us twenty-one horse-loads of bread and twenty-one cauldrons full of soup, and in case we fail to eat all at one meal they will refuse to give us the princess."

"Be of good cheer." said the ravenous eater; "I take the responsibility upon myself."

On the following day all the bread and soup was served to one man, and there was not enough to gratify him. He was still crying, "I am hungry! I am starving! Give me something to eat!"

"A plague upon these fellows!" said the King to his peers; "we could not satisfy one; what if all the seven should eat! Now I tell you what to do; entertain them in another house; bring quantities of wood and rushes at night and pile them round about the building, and in the middle of the night when they are asleep set fire to the piles. Thus they will perish and we shall get rid of them."

The ground-listener hearing everything, told it to the boy.

"Never mind," said the river-drinker, "I can keep in my stomach water enough to extinguish their fire."

He went and drank the neighboring river dry and came back, and all went to bed. At midnight they saw that the house was on fire. The river-drinker blew upon the flames, and lo! a stream of water began to flow from his mouth. It not only extinguished the flames, but drowned all those who were making the fire. That caused the King to be still more angry, and he said to his peers:

"Let come what may, I will not give up my daughter."

"Now it is my turn," said the earth-carrier, "if he does not give us his daughter I will carry away his whole kingdom."

He had hardly finished his words when he put his shoulder under the ground of the King of the East, and lo! He took on his back the whole realm. Then the shepherd began to blow his horn and the mountains and valleys, plains and forests, and all living creatures in them began to dance; the strider-of-the-world walked before them opening the way; and so the procession went on with great merriment. Thereupon the King began to weep and to beg them, saying:

"For heaven's sake, leave me my kingdom! take my daughter and go."

Then the earth-carrier set the kingdom down in its place again; the shepherd ceased blowing his horn, and the universe stopped dancing. The boy thanked his six brothers for their valuable services and sent them to their homes, and he himself took the maiden and came to the Prince's city, where a wedding festival was celebrated for forty days, and he married this maiden also. He sat down with the baby born during his absence, in his arms, and his two wives one on each side, and calling his father and mother to him, said:

"Now shall I tell you what my dream was?"

"Yes, what was it?" said his parents.

"I dreamed in my dream," said the boy, "that there was one sun upon my right side, another sun upon my left side, and a bright star was twinkling upon my heart."

"Was that your dream?" they said.

"Yes, that was my dream," he said.

This tale was a dream. The Sender of dreams has sent three apples from above—one for him who told the story, one for him who asked that the story be told, and one for him who listened to the story.

DYJHICON: THE COWARD-HERO

Dyjhicon was a poor unfortunate fellow who had only two goats and a cow. His wife was an ambitious woman, and annoyed him by her frequent demands.

"I want you to go out and work," she often said. "I want you to build a new house, I want to buy myself some new dresses, oxen and sheep, a horse and wagon."

Dyjhicon, tiring of her endless complaints and scoldings, one day took his great stick and drove the cow out of the house, saying to himself:

"Let me run from this wicked wife to the wilderness and there die."

This was what the woman wanted. Thus he ran from her and wandered in the wilderness. When he was hungry he milked the cow and drank the milk, and when he was tired he mounted the cow. He was very timid—a typical coward. The sight of a running rat was enough to make him tremble.

"Eh!" he thought, nevertheless, "it is better to be torn by wild beasts than to become the slave of a wicked woman."

One day, as the cow was pasturing on a green meadow and Dyjhicon was lying down lazily, the flies stung him. He cursed his wife and clapped his hands to kill the flies. Then he counted to see how many flies he had killed at one stroke, and lo! They were seven in number. This encouraged him, and he took his knife and carved upon his stick these words:

"I am Dyjhicon; I have killed seven by one stroke of the hand."

Then he got astride the cow and rode away. After a long journey he came to a green meadow in the center of which there was a magnificent castle with an orchard around it. He let the cow graze in the meadow and he lay down to sleep. Seven brothers lived in that castle. One of them, seeing Dyjhicon and his cow in the meadow came to find who it was that had ventured to enter their ground. Dyjhicon was sleeping, with his stick standing near him. The man approached and, reading the inscription, was terrified.

"What a hero!" he thought to himself, "he has killed seven men by one stroke of the hand. He must be a brave man, else he would not dare to sleep here so carelessly. What courage! What boldness! He has come so far without arms, without a horse, without a companion. This man is surely a great hero."

He went and informed his brothers as to what he had seen; and all the seven brothers came to pay their respects to the unknown hero, and to invite him to their humble home. The cow, being frightened by their approach, began to leap and bellow. Her voice wakened Dyjhicon, who, seeing seven men standing before him, was terrified, and snatching his club, stood aside trembling. The seven brothers thought that he was angry with them, and was trembling on account of his wrath, and that he would kill all of them by one stroke of his stick. Thereupon they began to supplicate him to pardon their rudeness in disturbing his repose. Then they invited him to go with them, saying:

"We are seven brothers and have a great reputation as good fighters in this district. But we shall be entirely invincible, if you will join us and become our elder brother. We will take great pleasure in placing our house and all that belongs to us at the service of such a hero as yourself."

Hearing this, Dyjhicon ceased trembling, and said:

"Very well, let it be as you say."

They took him to the castle with great pomp and served

to him a grand banquet, at which all the seven brothers stood before him, folding their arms upon their breasts and awaiting his permission to sit. Dyjhicon was in great alarm, his heart was faint and he had fallen into meditation as to the manner in which he might free himself from this perplexing situation. The seven brothers thought that he was not only a very brave hero, but was also such a great sage, that he did not care even to look at their faces. They began to cough in a low voice to draw his attention. On account of his internal fear Dyjhicon suddenly shook his head. The seven brothers took this as a permission to sit. After the banquet they said to him:

"My lord, where have you left your horse, arms and servants? Will you command us to go and bring them?"

"Horse and arms are necessary for timid men," said Dyjhicon; "I have never had need of them. I use horse and arms only when I fight a great battle. As to servants, I never need them; all men are my servants. You see, I have come so far having only a cow and my stick. Dyjhicon is my name; I have killed seven by one stroke of the hand."

Their esteem and admiration for Dyjhicon increased every day, and at last they were so much fascinated by his alleged bravery that they gave him in marriage their only sister, who was a very beautiful maiden. Dyjhicon knew that he was unworthy, but he could not refuse this gift.

"Eh!" he said, "I will do you the favor of marrying her since you entreat me so earnestly."

They brought costly garments, and putting them on Dyjhicon, made him a handsome bridegroom. They had a splendid wedding festival, talked about in all the neighboring countries. The four princes of the neighboring countries had asked the hand of the maiden in marriage, and all of them had been refused. Now hearing that the maiden was given in marriage to a stranger, the four princes waged war against the seven brothers. Dyjhicon, hearing this, was stricken with fear, and longed that the earth might open its mouth and swallow him. He thought to run away, but there were no means of escaping. While he indulged in these sad meditations, the seven brothers came, and bowing down before him, said:

"What is your order, my lord? Will you go fight yourself, or will you have us go first?"

This caused Dyjhicon's heart to melt. He began to tremble in his whole body, and to strike his teeth one against another. The seven brothers thought that it was because of his violent rage, and that in his fury he would destroy whole armies.

"My lord," they said, finally, "let us seven brothers go fight them at first, and if we find them hard to conquer we will send you word, that you may come to our assistance."

"Well, well; do so," answered Dyjhicon, somewhat relieved.

They went and began the battle. Their neighboring peoples were in constant terror of the seven brothers, who were famous as brave fighters. Now that they had also a brother-in-law who could kill seven men by one stroke of the hand, their foes were the more afraid of them. But this time the men of the four princes were united, and they fought with unusual zeal and determination. This caused the seven brothers to retreat a little, and they sent to brother Dyjhicon, saying:

"We are in trouble; come to our assistance."

A fast horse and magnificent arms awaited him. He began to curse the day when he came to that house. But what could he do now? At last he decided to go to the battlefield, cast himself against the swords of the enemy and die; death was preferable to such a disgraceful life. As soon as he mounted the horse, the beast, knowing that the rider was inexperienced, ran away like a winged eagle. Dyjhicon could not stop or manage it. The seven brothers thought he was so brave that he left the horse free in order to reach and slaughter the enemy. The horse broke into the line of the enemy, who began to fly, saying:

"Who can stand before this great hero?"

In their hurry to retreat they began to slaughter one another. Dyjhicon, who had never been on horseback before, was so much afraid that he thought he was already lost. As the horse was running through the forest, he threw his arms around an oak tree and embraced it, letting the horse go from under him. The tree happened to be rotten and was rooted out when he took hold of it. This caused a great panic among the enemy, who ran away exclaiming:

"Aha! He has pulled up by the roots an enormous oak, and now he means to batter us into pieces with it. Who can stand before this strong warrior?"

So crying as they ran away, they slaughtered one another. Thereupon, the seven brothers came and embracing the feet of their heroic brother-in-law, exclaimed:

"What magnificent courage! What a great victory!"

With these words they brought Dyjhicon home with great pomp and glory. The four princes who waged the war, being greatly humiliated, sued for reconciliation, and in order to gain Dyjhicon's favor, each of them sent him as a present one thousand ewes with their lambs, ten mares with their colts, and other costly offerings.

Thus the greatest coward became the greatest hero.

THE GOLDEN MAIDEN

Once upon a time there was a wicked widow who had an ugly daughter. She married a widower who had a beautiful daughter and a son by his first wife. The stepmother hated the two motherless children, and used every means to persuade her husband to take them away to the mountains and abandon them as a prey to wild beasts. The poor man loved his children, but being weak was unable to resist his wife's frequent threats. Therefore, one day he put bread in a bag, and took the two children up to the mountains. After a long journey they came to a lonely wilderness. The man said to the children:

"Sit here and take a little rest," and then, turning his face away, he began to sob bitterly.

"Father! Father, why are you weeping?" exclaimed the children, and they also began to weep.

The man opened the bag and gave them bread, which they soon ate.

"Father," said the boy, "I am thirsty."

The man drove his stick into the ground, and placing his cloak over the stick, said:

"Come, children, sit here under the shadow of this cloak; I will go and see if there is a fountain nearby."

The children sat under the cloak, while their father disappeared behind the trees and rocks.

After waiting a long time, the two innocent children grew tired and began to ramble about in search of their father, but in vain.

"Father! father!" they exclaimed, but only the echo of the mountains returned their answer—"Father! father!"

The children came back, crying: "Alas! The stick is here,

the cloak is here, but father is not here!"

Thus they cried for a long time, and seeing that nobody appeared, they got up, and one of them took the stick and the other the cloak and they began to wander about in the wilderness, not knowing where to go. After a long ramble, they came to a place where some rainwater had gathered on the ground in a print made by the hoof of a horse.

"Sister," said the little boy, "I am thirsty; I want to drink of this water."

"No," said the maiden, "do not drank of this water; as soon as you drink of it you will become a colt."

Soon they came to another print made by the hoof of an ox, and the boy said:

"Sister, I am thirsty; I want to drink."

But she would not let him drink, saying: "As soon as you drink of this water you will become a calf."

Then they came to another print made by the paw of a bear, and the boy wanted to drink; but his sister prevented him lest he should become a cub of a bear. Then they came to a track made by the foot of a pig, and the boy again wanted to drink, but the maiden prevented him, lest he should turn into a young pig. Soon they came to a print made by the foot of a wolf; but the boy did not yield till they came to one made by the hoof of a lamb.

"Sister," exclaimed the boy, "I am thirsty; I cannot wait any longer; I will drink from this no matter what."

"Alas!" said the maiden, "What can I do? I am ready to give my life to save you, but it is impossible. You will turn into a lamb the moment you drink of this water."

The boy drank, and was at once changed into a lamb, and began to follow his sister bleating. After a long and dangerous journey they found the way to the town, and came to their house. The stepmother was angry to see them come back, though one of them was now a lamb. As she had great influence over her husband, he used every means to please her. One day she said to him:

"I want to eat meat; you must kill your lamb that I may eat it."

The sister, hearing this, at once took her lamb-brother and fled secretly to the mountains, where, sitting on a high rock, she spun wool while the lamb grazed safely near her. As she was thus spinning, her spindle fell suddenly from her hand into a deep cave. The maiden, leaving the lamb grazing, went down to find her spindle. Entering the cave, she was surprised to see an old fairy woman, a thousand years of age, who perceiving the maiden, exclaimed: "Maiden, neither the bird with its wing, nor the snake on its belly can enter here; how could you venture to come here?"

The terrified maiden was at a loss for an answer, but she replied with a gentle voice: "Your love brought me here, grandmother."

The old fairy was pleased with this kind answer, and invited the maiden to have a seat beside herself, and inquired of her many things concerning the world outside. The more she talked with the maiden the better she liked her and she said:

"Now you are hungry; let me bring you some fishes to eat."

She went into the cave, and returned with a plateful of cooked snakes, at the sight of which the maiden shuddered with horror and began to weep.

"What is the matter?" inquired the old lady; "why are you weeping?"

"Nothing," answered the maiden, shyly; "I remembered my dead mother who was so fond of fish, and therefore I wept."

Then she told the old fairy her sad story, and the ill treatment of the wicked stepmother. The fairy woman was very much interested in the maiden's story, and said to her:

"Be seated, and let me sleep in your lap. In that fireplace there is a plowshare. When the Black Fairy passes do not wake me; but when the Red-and-Green Fairy passes, quickly press the red-hot plowshare on my feet, that I may awake."

The poor maiden shuddered with fear, but she could do nothing but consent. Accordingly the old fairy woman laid down in the maiden's lap and slept. Soon a fairy as black as night passed through the cave; but the maiden did not move. Then the Red-and-Green Fairy appeared and the whole cave was gilded with his radiant beams. The maiden immediately pressed the red-hot plowshare on the feet of the sleeping fairy woman, who immediately woke and exclaimed:

"Oh! What is biting my feet?"

The maiden told her that nothing had bitten her, but it was the red-hot plowshare she felt, and that it was time to get up. The old fairy rose and caused the maiden to stand up as the Red-and-Green Fairy proceeded, whose gleaming rays had such an effect upon her that her hair and garments were all turned to gold and she herself was turned into a fairy maiden. After the Red-and-Green Fairy disappeared, the maiden, kissing the fairy woman's hand, left the cave, and taking her lamb-brother, went home. Seeing that the stepmother was not at home, she at once took off her golden garments, hid them in a secret comer and put on her old rags. Soon the step-mother entered, and seeing the golden hair of the maiden, exclaimed:

"How now, little elf! What did you do to your hair to turn

it into gold?"

The maiden told her what had taken place. On the following day the stepmother sent her own daughter to the same spot. There, on purpose, she let her spindle fall, and entered the cave as if to pick it up. The fairy woman saw her, and taking a dislike to her, changed her into an ugly thing; so ugly, that it is impossible to describe her appearance. She came home, and the stepmother seeing her own daughter changed into a form of so great ugliness, was the more enraged at the two stepchildren.

One day the Prince of that country sent out messengers to proclaim all over his realm that his son was to be married, and that the most beautiful maiden in all the land should be his bride. He commanded all the marriageable maidens to assemble in the palace courtyard where the young Prince would make his selection. At the appointed time all the maidens of the land had crowded into the courtyard. The step-mother dressed her own daughter in the best garments and ornaments she could procure, veiling her ugly face very carefully, however, and took her to the courtyard, hoping that the Prince would select her to be his bride. In order to prevent her stepdaughter from appearing before the Prince, the stepmother scattered a measure of wheat in the yard, and bade the maiden to pick up the wheat before she returned, threatening to beat her to death if she failed to finish the task. After the stepmother went away, however, the maiden let loose the chickens, which quickly picked up the wheat to the very last grain; and she, putting on her golden garments, was changed to a fairy maiden so beautiful that she might say to the sun:

"Sun, you need not shine, for I am shining."

Then she went to the Prince's courtyard, where she was

the object of the admiration of the entire crowd. But she could not stay very long lest her step-mother should return first, and not finding her at home should beat her upon her return, so she ran hastily back, and hiding her golden garments put on her old rags. But in her haste she had dropped one of her golden slippers in the Prince's fountain.

Soon the young Prince, who had looked at the maidens without making a selection, came on horseback leading his animal to the fountain to water him; but the horse was frightened by the radiant beams from the slipper. The servants immediately entered the fountain, and taking out the slipper gave it to the Prince, who seeing it at once declared that the maiden who wore that slipper should be his bride. He and his peers began to search every house and to try the feet of the maidens to find the true owner of the slipper. They had just approached the house of the Golden Maiden, when the stepmother took her and hid her in the great kitchen pit, which is used as a furnace, presenting her own ugly daughter as the owner of the golden slipper. Of course, the slipper did not fit. As the Prince and his peers were leaving the house, the rooster flew from his roost, perched on the top of the door, and cried:

"Goo-goo-li-goo-goo! The Golden Maiden is in the pit!"

The pit was immediately opened, and lo! The maiden jumped out. The slipper fitted, and the maiden, taking out her golden garments and the second slipper from the corner where she had hid them, put them on, and was changed to a fairy maiden. The Prince seeing this embraced her as his bride. Taking the lamb-brother with them, they went to the Prince's palace, where their wedding was celebrated for seven days and seven nights.

One day the stepmother took her own daughter and went

to the Prince's palace to pay a visit to her stepdaughter, who conducted them to the Prince's orchard for a walk. As they came to the seashore, the stepmother said:

"Come, daughters, let us take a bath in the sea."

No sooner had they entered the sea, than the stepmother, intending to drown the golden bride, pushed her into the deep water. A great fish, however, chanced to be there and swallowed her. The stepmother at once gathered up the golden dresses of the bride, and putting them on her own ugly daughter, brought her to the palace. There she left her in the place of the golden bride, veiling carefully her ugly face.

The true bride remained in the belly of the fish for several days. One day, very early in the morning, she heard the sexton ringing the bell and inviting the people to church. She cried to him from the belly of the fish:

"Sexton! sexton! You ring your morning bell,
Crossing your face, send the devils to hell,
For God's sake, go to the young Prince and tell,
Let him not kill my lamb-brother, or sell."

The sexton, hearing this call repeated several times, went and informed the young Prince, who had by that time discovered the loss of his fairy bride. He immediately came to the seashore, where the sexton had heard the voice. Once more it was repeated, and the Prince recognized it as the voice of his bride. He drew his sword and leaped into the sea. Splitting the fish's belly, he drew out his bride, and taking her in his arms brought her to the palace. Soon he called the step-mother before him, saying:

"Now, kind mother, which gift do you prefer, a nimble-footed horse or a keen sword?"

"Let your keen sword stab your enemies," answered the stepmother, overjoyed with the expectation of a valuable present; "I will have the nimble-footed horse."

"I take you at your word," said the Prince; "you shall have the horse."

He ordered his men to bind the stepmother and her ugly daughter to the tail of a wild horse. Then the horse was whipped, and carried the two wicked women away to the mountains. They were thrown from stone to stone, and from tree to tree, until they were dashed into pieces.

The wicked persons being punished, the Prince celebrated a new wedding for forty days and forty nights, because he had found his lost golden bride. Being released from her rival, she thereafter enjoyed a happy life with her lamb-brother.

Three apples fell from Heaven—one for me, one for the story-teller, and one for him who entertained the company.

THE BETROTHED OF DESTINY

Once upon a time the King of the West had a son who, one night, dreamed a dream in which destiny betrothed him to the daughter of the King of the East. In the morning he awoke, and lo! The betrothal ring of the maiden was on his finger. On the very same night the same dream had come to the sleeping maiden, who the next day found on her finger the betrothal ring of the son of the King of the West. The boy started to look for his betrothed, and after a long journey came to the city of the King of the East. He entered into the service of the King as a stranger, because he could not make himself known on account of the constant strife between his father and the King of the East. He served the King seven years, during which he spent many happy hours with the young princess, his betrothed. At the expiration of the seven years he asked for the hand of the princess as remuneration for his services. The King, who was pleased with the boy, consented to give him his daughter in marriage. But the boy said he must take her to his country, where the wedding should take place. The King consented to that also, and let his daughter go, giving her a precious dowry. On their way to the country of the King of the West, they had to cross the sea, and so boarded a ship. The captain, being a wicked man, was charmed by the beauty of the maiden, and before the ship sailed he sent the boy ashore, bidding him to make further preparation, as the voyage would probably be long on account of contrary winds. As soon as the boy disappeared, the captain weighed anchor and set sail. The boy came back only to find that the ship had sailed away with his love on board. There remained nothing for him to do but to lament and bewail his bad luck. The maiden, who was in the cabin, did not discover the truth until it was too late. To her censure and upbraiding the vile captain answered with the proposal that she should become his wife.

"Marry such an ungracious beast as you!" she exclaimed. "I would rather make my grave in the unfathomable sea."

But the captain was strong, and they were on the open sea where no help could be expected. Seeing that she could not resist force if the captain resorted to it, she resolved to use craft.

"Well, then," she answered finally, "I will be your wife, but not upon the sea. We will go home to your city and there be married lawfully."

The captain consented, and they soon reached the city.

"Now, you go first," said the maiden, "and make preparation. I will wait here until you return."

Without suspicion the captain went ashore. As soon as he had disappeared the maiden lifted the anchor, and set sail without knowing where to go. At last she reached a certain city and cast anchor. The King of that city was a young boy of marriageable age, who was celebrating his wedding festival. Thirty-nine beautiful maidens were already elected; only one maiden was missing to complete the number forty from among whom he would choose his queen, while the others were to become handmaids to his new queen. The King, hearing that a beautiful maiden had come to the shore, hastened there and seeing the princess, said to her:

"Fair maiden, come and by your presence complete the number forty. You are the jewel of all the maidens, and will surely be my dear queen, while the rest shall become your handmaids."

"Very well, I will come," answered the princess; "only send your thirty-nine maidens here, so that I may come to your palace with great pomp."

The youthful King consented and sent his maidens on board the ship. As soon as they came, the princess weighed anchor and set sail. She told the thirty-nine maidens who she was, and asked them to accompany her until destiny showed them what to do. The maidens were fascinated by her beauty and commanding appearance, and promised to follow her wherever she went, even to the end of the earth. After sailing for a long time, they came to an unknown shore where there was a castle. They cast anchor and landed. Entering the castle, they found in it forty rooms with a bed in each, all richly decorated. The castle contained great wealth and abundant food. Satisfying their hunger, they went to bed, each maiden occupying a chamber. In the middle of the night the door of the castle suddenly opened, and there entered forty brigands, who were the owners of the stronghold, and who were just returning from a nightly foray, bringing with them great booty.

"Aha!" exclaimed the brigands, seeing the maidens, "we hunted elsewhere, and lo! The antelopes have come to our own home."

"Enter, you brave heroes," said the maidens; "we were waiting for you."

And they pretended to be very much pleased to see the brigands, who entered the rooms occupied by the maidens without suspicion. When they had laid down their arms and retired to rest, each maiden took the sword of the brigand who lay in her room and cut off his head. Thus the maidens were the owners of their wealth and property. In the morning the maidens rose, and putting on the clothes and arms of the robbers, appeared as youthful knights. They mounted the brigands' horses, taking in their saddlebags gold, silver, jewels and other portable wealth. After a long journey they came to the city of the King of the West, and encamped in a meadow on the outskirts of the city. Soon they heard a herald crying that on the following day there should be elected a King of the realm, for inasmuch as the late sovereign had died and the heir-apparent was lost, it was necessary to choose a new ruler. On the following day all the people of the realm were gathered in the park adjoining the palace; the forty strangers also went to gratify their curiosity. Soon the nobles let loose the royal eagle, which flapped its wings and soared over the immense crowd, as though searching with its keen eyes for the true candidate for the throne. The multitude held their breath and stood still. The royal bird once more flapped its wings, and descending from its towering flight, perched upon the head of the princess, who was disguised as a knight.

"That is a mistake," exclaimed the noblemen; "we must try it again."

Once more they let loose the royal eagle, but again it alighted upon the head of the same stranger. A third trial gave the same result. Thereupon all the multitude saluted the disguised princess, the elect of destiny, exclaiming with one voice: "Long live the King!" And with great pomp they took her and her companions to the royal palace, where the princess was anointed with holy oil, and crowned King over the realm, and her companions were made ministers.

This new King proved to be the wisest and most just ruler that that country had ever enjoyed, and all the people of the realm loved and honored their sovereign with all their hearts. She built a splendid fountain in the midst of the city, on which she caused her image to be carved, so that every one who came to drink might see it. She put guards to watch the fountain day and night, and said to them:

"Watch carefully, and when you perceive a stranger who, on seeing my image, shows signs of knowing me, bring him hither."

One day there came a stranger who, after drinking, raised his eyes and saw the image. He gazed for a long time, and sighed deeply. Immediately he was arrested and taken to the King, who, looking at him from behind a curtain, ordered him to be imprisoned. This was the captain of the ship. On another day there came another stranger, and he also sighed. It was the King, the owner of the thirty-nine maidens. He was kept in an apartment of the palace. And at last, disguised as a stranger, came the Prince, the betrothed of the ruling sovereign, and the heir-apparent to the crown. He also looked at the image and sighed, and was taken to the palace. Thereupon the princess summoned a parliament of all the nobility and the learned and wise men of the realm. She caused the three strangers to be brought before the assembly, and told her story from beginning to end.

The captain was condemned to be hanged, and was executed. The lord of the thirty-nine maidens received them all, to whose number the princess added one of her most beautiful handmaids, thus making up the forty. The prince and the princess, the betrothed of destiny, celebrated their wedding with great joy and pomp for forty days and forty nights. The prince, as the true heir, was crowned King, his consort became Queen, and they reigned together.

Thus they reached their desire. May all of us attain our desires and the happiness ordained to us by an all-wise Providence.

Three apples fell from Heaven—one for me, one for the story-teller, and one for him who entertained the company.

ZOOLVISIA

Once upon a time there was a King who was very fond of hunting. He had extensive forests full of all kinds of game. But at the farthest boundaries of his dominions was a strip of land, surrounded by steep hills, which the people of the country considered enchanted ground, because no one who had gone there for the purpose of hunting had ever returned. One day the King said to his noblemen:

"Let us go and see what is there."

His men asked him to be advised and not to go. But the King insisted; they started upon the fatal journey and never came back. The King had two sons, the eldest of whom succeeded him. One day the younger brother said to the new King:

"I will go and avenge our father's death."

The King tried to dissuade him, but in vain; the boy insisted. He had some very faithful servants who said they would accompany him, and they all set out upon the perilous journey. As soon as they entered the enchanted ground they saw a beautiful antelope running before them. They began to chase the animal, which seemed to mock them with its graceful bounds over the bushes and rocks. They continued chasing it until late in the day, when they came to a thick forest surrounded by steep rocks. The antelope leaped over the rocks and disappeared in the forest. But the hunters' horses could go no farther, and they all dismounted. They were surprised to find an elegant tent pitched among the trees beside a fountain of pure water. Entering the tent, they saw a table spread with all kinds of delicious foods. They were very hungry and began to devour the food with ravenous appetites; after that they quenched their thirst from the crystal waters of the fountain. But the boy never tasted the food or the water; he thought to himself that there must be some deviltry at the bottom of this banquet. While his men gave themselves up to eating and drinking, the boy occupied himself in examining the neighborhood. To his great terror he saw not far from the tent a heap of human skeletons bleached and showing their grinning teeth. What could these be if not the bones of those who, from time to time, had come to hunt in that enchanted ground and been lost? Among these, perchance, were the bones of his own father. How could he have been killed? With these thoughts he came back to the tent, and to his great horror and grief saw that some of his men were already dead and others were breathing their last. He wished to help them, but in vain; they were soon as dead as stones. He could plainly see the cause; both the food and the water were poisoned. He now understood how all human beings who hunted in this region were done away with and heaped up on the pile of skeletons. But who was the perpetrator of this devilish crime? His blood began to boil, and he determined to do battle with the perpetrator whether human being, fairy or demon, until he had revenged the victims of this diabolical plot. He was buried in this meditation when he heard the footsteps of approaching horsemen, and he immediately withdrew to the depths of the forest, bound his horse to a sycamore tree, and concealed himself behind the bushes, whence he could see the tent and the neighborhood without himself being perceived. Soon a number of horsemen arrived, who appeared to be greatly pleased at seeing the dead men, and at once began to strip them of their clothes. They loaded each man's property upon his own horse, and prepared to drive the horses away. One of the riders, who no doubt was their leader, wore a complete suit of white armor, had locks of long hair and a graceful countenance, feminine in its beauty. The boy, who was watching them closely, took aim with his bow and arrow and was just about to shoot the leader in the forehead, when he suddenly stopped.

"That is a woman," he said to himself. "I will not shoot at a woman." At once he jumped out from the place of his concealment and standing before the leader exclaimed:

"Are you a human being, a fairy or a demon? Disclose yourself. To lead people astray and to destroy human life by poison are not the deeds of heroes. Come, let me measure swords with you."

These words of the boy at first called forth expressions of rage upon the countenance of the leader. But the next second the natural feminine grace again bloomed upon her cheeks, and she answered with a sweet musical voice, the sweetest that ever fell upon a human ear:

"Youth, I spare your life provided that your heart is as brave as your words. Zoolvisia is my name. If you want to show your courage before me, you must come where I live."

And she spurred her horse, and galloping disappeared behind the trees and rocks. The boy stood stone still as if struck by lightning. The beauty of the horsewoman had charmed him; her face was of light, her hair of gold, her horse of lightning. Was she a maiden?

"Zoolvisia! Zoolvisia!" the boy exclaimed suddenly, "I will find you."

And at once he mounted his horse and started in the direction whither Zoolvisia and her followers had gone. It was late in the evening, the sun having long before disappeared behind the horizon. After groping his way in the darkness for a while, he saw a light gleaming at a distance and turned his horse in that direction. When he arrived he saw a cave where a fairy woman was kneading dough.

"The goodness of the hour upon you, mother!" said the boy.

"Heaven bless you, son!" said the old lady. "Neither the snake on its belly, nor the bird with its wing could come here; why did you venture to come?"

"Your love brought me here, mother," answered the boy.

The fairy woman was pleased with the boy, and said to him:

"The seven fairies, my sons, have just gone out hunting; they hunt all night long and come back in the morning. If they find you here they will devour you. Let me hide you."

So speaking, she hid the boy in a hole near the cave. At daybreak the seven fairies returned, and smelling a human being, exclaimed:

"O mother! Last night you ate a human being; have you not kept at least some bones for us to pick?"

"I have eaten no human being," said their mother; "but my nephew, the son of a human sister, has come to visit us."

"Where is he, mother? We want to see our human cousin," said the fairies.

The old woman brought the boy out from the hole and presented him to the fairies, who were much pleased with him and asked him the reason for his journey. The boy said that he was going after Zoolvisia.

"Zoolvisia!" exclaimed the seven brothers. "Be advised, cousin, do not go. This is a most dangerous journey. Zoolvisia is a cruel tyrant. No human being who has ever undertaken this journey has returned. Come, cousin, stay with us; be our elder brother, we your subordinates, and let us live together in happiness."

"No," said the boy, "let come what may; I will go." Thereupon he gave the seven brothers a pair of scissors, saying:

"When you see blood dripping from the scissors, know that I am in danger and come to my rescue."

And he took leave of his adopted cousins. On his way he came to another cave where seven fairies lived with their mother, the sister of the former fairy woman, who accepted him as their cousin and tried to dissuade him from going. He gave to them a looking-glass, saying:

"When you see the glass covered with sweat, know that I am in trouble, and hasten to my rescue."

Then he came to a third house, where seven fairies lived with their mother, who was a sister of the former two. They also accepted him as cousin, and sought to dissuade him from going. He gave them a razor, saying:

"When you see drops of blood falling from the edge of this razor, know that my life is in danger, and run to my rescue."

Departing on his way he met an old monk in a cottage, who also tried to dissuade him; but as the boy insisted, the monk said:

"Let me advise you; Zoolvisia is the most beautiful maiden in the world. She is a princess endowed from above with a talisman. She has forty maids under her command who play the part of Amazons. She goes up to the top of the tower of her castle every morning at daybreak, dressed in her robe of pearls. Thence she gazes all about her realm, to see whether human beings or genii have trespassed upon her boundaries. Three times she cries out with a loud voice, and all who have been on her ground, on hearing her voice immediately drop dead as if struck by lightning. It is she who, taking the shape of an antelope, leads hunters astray and destroys them by poisonous food and water. Now, do as I advise you. As soon as you reach the vicinity of her castle, set up a stick and put on it your cloak and cap, and dig a trench in the neighborhood and conceal yourself, at the same time sealing both your ears with beeswax, so that no sound can penetrate them. At the beginning of daybreak watch her on the top of the tower. Do not stir at her first or second call, but as soon as her third call has ended, jump up from your place of concealment and stand before her. By this means you will break her talisman, and subdue her."

The boy thanked the old monk, and continuing his journey saw, at a distance, Zoolvisia's magnificent castle decorated with gold and jewels. He did just as the monk had advised him, and at Zoolvisia's third call jumped up and stood before her gazing at her. Zoolvisia recognized him, and said:

"You have overcome me; you are brave and a real hero worthy of me. No one except you has ever heard my voice and lived. Now my talisman is broken, and I have become a mere woman. Come in, hero, I and my forty maids will serve you."

The boy's heart began to yearn. All the hatred he cherished toward her who had perpetrated such terrible crimes had vanished. He had fallen in love with her, and Zoolvisia on her part loved the boy. She let the rich locks of her golden hair hang down from the window. The boy approached, took hold of them and kissed them, and lo! He was drawn up to the castle by them. They accepted one another as husband and wife, and celebrated their wedding for forty days and nights. The forty maids served them. At the end of forty days

Zoolvisia presented to the boy her horse of lightning. The animal seemed to be greatly pleased with his new master. The boy mounted the steed and prepared to go hunting when Zoolvisia gave him as a keepsake one of the locks of her hair in a pearl box. So the boy continued to hunt every day. One day, as he was chasing a deer on the precipitous borders of the river, the pearl box fell into the water and disappeared. The boy was sorry, but he could not help it, and came home without it. The pearl box was carried by the current of the river to the country of the King of the East, where the King's fishermen drew it from the water and took it to their master. The King, opening the box, was surprised to see the lock of golden hair. He called his noblemen and peers in council, and placing the box before them, said:

"You must tell me whose hair this is. If you do not give me an answer in three days I will cut off your heads."

"Long live the King!" answered the men. "In three days we will bring you word."

They met and asked the advice of all the learned men and magicians of the country, but in vain; they could not solve the riddle within the three days. On the third day, a witch hearing of the case came to the King's noblemen, saying:

"I can tell you what it is, but what will you give me?"

"If you save our heads," said the noblemen, "every one of us will give you a handful of gold coins."

The witch consented, took the gold and told them of Zoolvisia and her golden hair. The men told the King what they had heard from the witch, at the same time boasting that it was they who solved the riddle.

"Well, then," said the King, "I wish you to bring me Zoolvisia. I desire to marry her. I give you forty days' grace; if you do not bring her by that time I will cut off your heads."

The men at once went to the witch, saying:

"Witch, it is only you who can accomplish this and save our heads. We will give you whatever you demand if you will bring Zoolvisia."

The witch promised. Immediately she caught a score of snakes, and putting them in a large pitcher, corked its mouth. She then made a whip of a great black snake, and mounting upon the pitcher, gave it three blows. Thereupon the pitcher began to fly through the sky as if it had wings, with the witch on its back. Soon she came to Zoolvisia's garden, and hiding the pitcher under the weeds, she went and sat on the roadside where the boy would pass on his way from hunting. She had intentionally put on her torn dress, and her worn and dusty shoes. In the evening, the boy seeing her asked her who she was and how she had come there.

"O son!" the witch exclaimed with a pitiful voice, "may Heaven bless you! I am a pilgrim to Jerusalem. I missed the caravan and went astray; seeing your house at a distance, I came to take rest. For Heaven's sake, give me bread and water, and let me lodge with your dog at your gate."

The boy had compassion on her and took her on the back of his horse. But the wise animal knew by instinct that she was a wicked woman, and standing on his hind legs, caused her to fall down.

"I will follow slowly, son," said the witch. "Do you go ahead with your horse."

Zoolvisia, hearing that the boy had brought an old woman, said:

"Don't let her enter our house; she may be a witch and bring calamity upon us."

The boy gave orders to the maids to keep the old woman apart and not let her appear before Zoolvisia. But the witch was clever, and soon won the favor of the maids, who praised her before their mistress and asked her for the sake of merriment to summon her to her presence, at least once. She consented, and the witch was brought before her. The witch had a thousand and one ways of winning a young woman, and she soon became a great favorite with Zoolvisia, who could not spend an hour without her. One day she said to Zoolvisia:

"Blessed are you that have for a husband such a hero, who encounters and overcomes all, and himself is never destroyed. He discovered your secret, broke your talisman, and won your love. Of course you know his secret of bravery. May Heaven preserve his life! But can you tell me what his secret is?"

"No," answered Zoolvisia, "I don't know what his secret is."

"What sort of a husband and wife are you?" said the witch, scornfully. "He knows your secret, and you do not know his; and he says he loves you. Strange, strange!"

These words were enough to excite the curiosity of Zoolvisia, who in the evening again and again insisted to the boy, until he was induced to tell her that the secret of his bravery was his magic dagger, which he carried in his belt in daytime and put under his pillow at night. As soon as that dagger was taken away, he would lose all his power. With that they exchanged vows that nobody should know the secret, and also they exchanged rings as a sign to be true to one another, even to death. But woman is frail. On the following day Zoolvisia told the secret to the witch, adding:

"I have told you this to show you how my husband loves

me from his heart."

But she did not tell her anything in regard to the vows and exchange of rings. On that night the witch, using her craft, caused a heavy sleep to fall on all the inmates of the house. At midnight she entered the boy's room, and taking the magic dagger from under his pillow, threw it from the window into the neighboring pond. Then she went to bed and pretended to sleep. In the morning Zoolvisia and the maids saw that their master did not rise. They entered the room, and lo! The boy had fallen from his bed and lay benumbed, foaming at the mouth. They called him; but there was no answer.

"Look under the pillow and see whether the magic dagger is there," exclaimed Zoolvisia. They looked, and lo! It had been stolen. Then they all began to wail and cry. Thereupon the witch came in to see if the boy was really dead. She beat her breast, she beat her knees, she pulled her hair, crying and yelling all the time. Then she went out, brought the pitcher to the door of the castle, and re-entered surrounded by scores of snakes, which were hissing with their forked tongues. All were stricken with terror and began to scream and yell. She bade the snakes bite the maidens, who all fell down in a swoon. Then she said to Zoolvisia:

"Now you must obey me and come with me, else I will set on you all these snakes, which will bite you and tear you into pieces."

Zoolvisia was terrified and mute. The witch pushed her down the stairs, and thrusting her into the pitcher, shut its mouth. She then mounted the pitcher, and gave three strokes with the snake whip, which caused it to fly. She alighted in the country of the King of the East, and taking Zoolvisia out, gave her to the King's ministers, who paid her with a horse-load of gold. Zoolvisia was taken to the King's palace.

Let us return to the boy. The twenty-one fairies, the boy's adopted cousins, seeing that blood was dripping from the scissors and the razor, and that the looking glass was covered with sweat, understood that their human kinsman was in danger, and hastened to his rescue. Reaching the castle they saw the boy still in torpor, and the maids covered with snakes. On killing the snakes, all the maids revived, and told the fairies what had happened. They looked everywhere for the dagger, but in vain. In the evening they were all hungry, but there was nothing at home to eat. The fairies, seeing that large fishes were swimming in the pond, dove in and threw the fishes ashore. A great fish being thrown ashore was divided into two halves, and lo! The magic dagger fell out. The fish had swallowed it. The moment the dagger was put under the boy's pillow he jumped up, washed himself, and was surprised to see that his fairy cousins had come. They told him everything. Immediately he ran to the stable. The horse was there, but in a pitiable condition; it had neither eaten nor drunk; it had fallen in the dust. As soon as the animal saw the boy and smelled him it jumped up, neighing. The boy gave it food to eat and water to drink, brushed it clean, and kissing it on the forehead, said:

"O my wise horse! You foresaw the calamity by your unerring instinct, for you threw the hag from your back, and lo! What she has brought upon us. Now let us go after Zoolvisia."

The animal, as if understanding what the boy said, neighed and beat the ground with its hoofs, and seemed to say, "Yes, let us go; I am ready to go."

The boy came back to the castle, gave to the maidens many precious presents, and sent them away free. He gave the castle and the treasures in it to the fairies, himself taking only his saddlebags full of gold coins. He mounted the horse and went down the river until he came to the city of the King of the East. He stopped before the cottage of an old woman on the outskirts of the city and knocked at the door.

"Have you a night's lodging for me, mother?" asked the boy.

"No, master, I have no place for you," answered the lady. "You had better go elsewhere."

"Here is something for you," said the boy, giving her a handful of gold. "You are the crown of my head, son!" exclaimed the old woman. "I have room both for you and your horse."

The boy entered in to lodge. After the meal he asked the old woman in regard to the news in the city, and was told that Zoolvisia was in the King's palace, where for thirty-five days there had been a wedding festival, and after five days she would be married to the King. But she had said to the King that she did not wish to marry him, as she was the wife of some one else, and that rather than to be forced to it she would die by drinking poison, which she had ready in her hand. She therefore received nobody.

"Well, well, mother; that is enough," said the boy. "You keep a secret, don't you?"

"Oh, better than you desire," answered the old woman.

"Here is another handful of gold coins," said the boy; "go to the market place and buy a suit of costly garments. Put them on, and go and see Zoolvisia. Take this ring, put it on your finger, and show it to her; then bring me word what she says."

The old woman did just as he had told her. The palace servants thought she was the wife of the prime minister, and told Zoolvisia that the greatest lady in the realm had come to visit her.

"I don't want her, I don't!" cried Zoolvisia; "Let her not come near me."

The old woman did not pay any attention to the words of the servants, who told her that Zoolvisia did not want to see her, but pushed on and opened the door of the room where Zoolvisia was confined, and held the ring before her eyes. As soon as Zoolvisia caught a glance of the ring, she became as tame as a lamb.

"You are welcome, kind lady!" she exclaimed, with her sweet voice, "please be seated," and she shut the door. When they were alone she said:

"Where is the owner of that ring, mother?"

"He is a guest in my house," replied the woman, "and is waiting to know your will."

"Go tell him," said Zoolvisia, "to rest for three days. Do you immediately go to the King, and say that you have persuaded me to become his wife. Let him be of good cheer. On the third day I shall go for recreation to the public garden. It is the business of your guest to do the rest. Farewell!"

"Farewell!" said the old woman, and went directly to the King's apartment, saying proudly that she had persuaded Zoolvisia, who early on the third day would go to the public garden for recreation, and when she returned would become his wife. The King was delighted, and gave the old woman costly presents. She came and told her guest all that had happened. Early on the third day, as Zoolvisia had gone to the public garden with great pomp, the boy came on the back of his horse like a flash of lightning, put his arm about Zoolvisia's waist, and in the twinkling of an eye, disappeared. The crowd thought it was a hurricane, and all were stricken with terror. As soon as the King and his men realized the fact that she had been taken away, they mounted their horses and started in pursuit of the unknown horseman. The boy, having put Zoolvisia in a safe place, came back with his horse of lightning, killed the King and his favorites with his magic dagger, and told the crowd in the public garden who he was. The people, who were tired of their tyrannical King, prayed that he would become their King and Zoolvisia their Queen. The boy went and brought Zoolvisia back. A crowd conducted them with great pomp to the throne, where they are still reigning as King and Queen.

Three apples fell from heaven—one for me, one for the story-teller, and one for him who entertained the company.

DRAGON-CHILD AND SUN-CHILD

There was once a King who had no children, and whose life was very desolate. He asked the advice of all the doctors and learned men of his realm to relieve him of his trouble, but it was of no avail. In order to forget his dejected condition, he gave his time to hunting. One day, as he was walking in the forest he saw a snake coiled in the sun, surrounded by its little ones. For a long time he gazed wistfully at this family circle, and recognizing that his condition was inferior to that of the reptile parent, he sighed deeply and complained to Heaven, saying:

"O Heaven! Have I not so much value before you as this reptile, that you torment me by denying to me offspring and happiness?"

He never forgot the sight of this snake-family. One day a child came to the palace, but it was a monster, half man and half dragon. Now the grief of the King was heavier than before. They could not kill the monster because it was of royal birth. They therefore cast the Dragon-child into a dry well, where they fed him a cup of goat's milk every day. Soon the Dragon-child grew and required meat for his diet. Then they cast to him, every week, a tender girl; and when he grew older, they gave him a maiden to devour. Every house of the land furnished a maiden for the Dragon-child. It came the turn of a poor man who, being a widower, had a daughter from his former wife, and had married a widow who had a daughter of her own. The husband said that they must cast the wife's daughter to the Dragon-child, but his wife insisted that they must cast the husband's daughter. The woman's will was followed and so the stepmother prepared her stepdaughter to be cast to the Dragon-child on the following day. The maiden was very beautiful and graceful. She wept all night and prayed God to pity her. At midnight she heard some one speak to her in her dreams, saying:

"Maiden, do not fear being cast to the Dragon-child. Tell your father to send with you three cups of the milk of a black goat, and do you provide a knife for yourself. Let your father wrap you in a bull's skin and lower you and the milk by a rope into the well. When the Dragon-child bids you come out from the bull's skin in order that he may devour you, tell him to come out from the dragon's skin, that you may bathe him with milk. When he comes out, do you also cut the bull's skin with your knife and come out of the skin and bathe him."

On the following morning the maiden told her dream to her father, who got the required things ready, at the same time praying Heaven that what the maiden had dreamed might come true. The maiden being lowered into the well, the Dragon child bade her come out of the bull's skin; to which the maiden answered as she was advised. Thereupon in its fury, the dragon's skin burst, and lo! A handsome boy came out. The maiden cut the bull's skin with her knife, in a hurry to emerge, but in her haste she fell down, and one of her front teeth was broken. She bathed the boy with goat's milk and he became a sound, gallant youth, who at once expressed his gratitude to her for releasing him from his horrible bondage. Just then the maiden's father came to the mouth of the well, to see whether her dream was true or false, and perceiving them, ran to inform the King, who hastened to the spot accompanied by the Queen and his peers. They drew the Dragon-child and his deliverer from the well with great joy and ceremony.

They celebrated a wedding festival for forty days and nights, and the youth and the maiden loved one another and were married.

It came to pass, after a time that on account of a war the Dragon-child had to go away from home. When he was about departing he asked his mother not to send his bride away, not even to her father's, lest some misfortune should befall her. The Queen promised. But a thousand devils had entered the heart of the bride's stepmother, who was jealous of her good luck. She came and invited the bride to their house, saying that both she and her husband were longing to see her. When this was refused she sent her husband, who urgently entreated the Queen to send his daughter to his house at least for one day. The Queen thought there could be no harm in this, and so she let the bride go. The stepmother took her daughter and the bride for a walk on the seashore. When they came there she said to them:

"Daughters, let us bathe."

They entered the sea to bathe. The wicked woman, pretending to help the bride, took her toward the deep sea, where she gave her a violent push and she was caught by the waves and was drawn by the current out to the open sea. When she was sure that the bride had been drowned, she hastened to the shore with her own daughter, and putting the bride's dress on the latter, sent her to the King's palace as the true bride.

Let us turn to the fortunes of the maiden in the sea. For a long time she struggled against the violent waves, and was saved from being drowned by catching hold of an empty cask that happened to float near her. The wind blew from the shore, and the current carried the cask and the maiden away to the open sea. For three days and nights she floated with the cask, and then she was cast upon an uninhabited shore. She walked for a time on the coast, but saw no sign of a human being. She was hungry, naked and very tired. The first thing she did was to gather rushes and moss and weave for herself something like an apron to hide her nakedness. She then gathered wild berries and ate, and quenched her thirst from a brook nearby. While she was lingering on the banks of the brook she noticed a small hut hidden among the bulrushes and weeds. Proceeding thither, she looked in, and lo! a boy was sleeping in the hut. She sat down near the door of the hut. Soon after sunset the boy awoke, and as he was coming out of the hut, he noticed the maiden. Thinking that she was a fairy or a demon, he made upon his face the sign of the cross, at the same time stepping backward. But to his surprise, seeing that she did not vanish, he said to her:

"Are you a fairy, a demon or a human being? Disclose yourself."

The maiden told him her story.

"My own story is as strange as yours," then said the boy. "I was the only son of a rich man and had plenty to spend and enjoy. I led a dissipated life and went hunting every day. Once it happened that I did not shoot any game for three days in succession. I was enraged to the verge of madness, and wandered all the night. At daybreak my madness reached its climax, and I resolved to shoot the sun and drop him dead from his orb that darkness might cover the world, since I could take no game and have no pleasure. At once I grasped my bow and arrow, took aim at the sun, who had just lifted his shining face from behind the hills, and had hardly loosed the bowstring when I felt a blazing palm slap me in the face; a hand of fire took hold of my hair and cast me into this wilderness, and I heard an angry voice thundering at me from the overhanging clouds, declaring that I was cursed and should never see the light of the sun any more. I thus remain abandoned here, and sleep in the hut all the day while the sun shines, and go out only at night to procure food. If I go out of this hut after day-break I am doomed to die a horrible death."

As fate had so strangely cast these two youthful beings into the same lonely place, they decided to live together, accepting one another as husband and wife. Thus she who had been the consort of the Dragon-child was now the companion of the Sun-child. The woman worked in the daytime, and the man at night, and so they earned their living. But soon married life brought a change upon the woman, who needed the help of others, and they decided that she must go to the parents of the Sun-child. The boy wrote the following letter to his parents:

"I herewith send you your daughter-in-law; keep her and take care of her as my wife. But do not seek me; I cannot see the sun, I cannot come home, neither can I enter the city. If I do come I shall surely die; I am cursed."

Walking during the nights, and hiding himself in caves in daytime, the boy brought his wife to the vicinity of his parents' house, and himself went back to his lonely hut. The woman gave the letter to her father-in-law, and was accepted. The boy's father and mother hearing that their son was alive, said they would go and bring him, but the bride dissuaded them, saying that they would be the means of his death. In the fullness of time the family was cheered by the birth of a son, which the young mother put in a cradle and rocked, singing to it melodious lullabies from the incidents of her own life. One night as the young mother was putting her baby to sleep, another voice was heard out in the darkness singing a melodious lullaby. The bride recognized the voice to be that of the Sun-child, who had come from such a great distance, being drawn by the love of the baby; but he could not enter. This was repeated several times until the bride's father and mother-in-law heard that somebody was in the habit of coming at night, and singing lullabies by turns with their daughter-in-law. Suspicion entered into their minds that the bride might have a lover who was making nightly calls on her. The young woman, seeing that they were watching her with mistrust, said:

"It is your son who comes and sings lullabies; the love which he bears to the baby draws him, but he cannot enter; the moment you compel him to come in he dies."

"Nay, you are lying!" exclaimed her father and mother-in-law with rage; "there must be some foul play here. We will keep watch and catch the nightly visitor; if he proves to be our son, well and good; if not, woe be unto you."

That night they kept watch, and when the voice from outside was heard they ran and took hold of the man, and lo! it was their son, who begged them, saying:

"For Heaven's sake, let me go! If by the time the sun rises I am not hid in my hut, I die. Spare my life; I am cursed!"

This sounded to his father and mother like deceit, and they kept him at home until daybreak. As soon as the first rays of the sun beamed from the East, lo! The boy sank in the arms of his father and mother, and died. He died, but strange to say, his spirit did not depart from him entirely. They said he would revive at sunset. But not so; at night also he was in the same benumbed state. The house was changed into a house of sorrow; but worse than that befell. He was not dead so that they could bury him and he was not alive so that they might talk with him or administer a remedy. The parents took stones and beat their own heads, they pulled their hair, and sat in ashes and sackcloth. They lamented and wailed, but it was all of no avail. One night the afflicted mother dreamed a dream in which this revelation was made to her:

"Get up, put on iron sandals, take in your hand an iron rod and travel toward the West, until your sandals are worn and your rod is broken. Wherever holes are opened in your sandals and your rod is broken, there you will find a remedy for your son."

There is no limit to a mother's love and pity. As soon as she awoke in the morning she ordered the blacksmith to make her a pair of iron sandals and an iron rod, and she set out toward the West, walking day and night. She travelled through the countries of white men, red men, black men; she passed through the lands of fairies, giants and genii: she went farther than beasts and birds would dare to go; she had gone to the very limits of the earth. There she saw at a distance a palace built of blue marble, whither she proceeded. Before the palace door the iron rod fell from her hand and was broken; she got out her sandals to shake off the dust, and lo! they were worn and there was a hole in each. She said to herself:

"It is here that I shall find a remedy for my son!"

She entered and passed through twelve courtyards in succession. Each courtyard was surrounded by four arches, where thousands of myriads of stars were sleeping. At the center of each courtyard there was a marble pond with a stream of crystal water gushing from an orifice. There were no trees, no grass, no birds, no beasts, and no other creature. A deep silence was reigning everywhere. Upon the pond in the middle courtyard there were four golden arches, upon which there was a golden room of great splendor with a pearl bed in the center. Near the window there was, sitting upon a golden throne, a Queen so fair and beautiful, that no human being can describe her loveliness. From head to foot she was covered with diamonds and her face beamed with rays of light. At sight of this grandeur the poor woman was greatly amazed; she turned pale and began to shiver like an autumn leaf before a cold blast from the North. She fell upon her knees, and lifting her hands, was about to speak, when suddenly the Queen interrupted her, saying:

"Human being, Heaven has never permitted a member of the human race to enter this palace before. As you are the first mortal who has been allowed to come so far, you must have some valid reason. From your appearance I judge that you are a mother and have some maternal grief. Tell it to me; be not afraid."

These words of the Queen encouraged the woman, who said:

"Long live the Queen! Yes, I am a mother, and have travelled so far to ask the life of my only son."

And she told her story, to which the Queen made answer:

"Your son was an evil boy. I am a mother myself. The Sun is my son, by whose living rays heaven and earth are illumined. Your son was so wicked that he wanted to shoot my son, the giver of life to the universe. All kinds of sins may be pardonable to a man, but a sin against the sole source of life is not pardonable. Your son was therefore doomed to be deprived of life. He is cursed. He will live, but not live; he will die, but not die."

"I am a mother," repeated the woman, "come to beg the life of my son. I have come so far that my iron sandals are worn out, and my iron rod is broken. I would willingly go still further if it were necessary. For the love you bear your son, O Queen of this luminous orb, devise a remedy for my grief!"

These words served to arouse the compassion of the Queen, who replied:

"There are very many unworthy children who enjoy life simply because of their virtuous mothers. Let it be so with your son, O virtuous woman, who bear such great maternal love in your heart! Now, go hide yourself behind yonder stars. The day is growing towards evening and my son will soon be here; if you do not hide yourself you will be burned. The first thing he does after reaching this place is to dive in this pond; then he comes to be nursed from my breast. Just then take a bottle full of the water of the pond where he has been washing, and carry it home. As soon as you sprinkle that water upon your son he will be healed."

Soon the Sun came embodied in flames. The Stars waked and stood on their feet for a time to salute their mighty King; then they scattered over the surface of the blue dome to twinkle in their respective orbits, because it was night. The Sun dove into the pond, and the Queen stretching out her hand took him out of the water. She placed him in the bed of pearl and began to nurse him, for the Sun, who never wears out, never grows old, is a baby from everlasting to everlasting. The woman came out from her concealment and taking a bottle of water from the pond, quickly retraced her steps. She arrived safely at her home, and sprinkled the water upon her son, who was healed. The report of this most wonderful journey of the woman was published all over the world, and princes and philosophers came from distant countries and from the ends of the earth to see the woman and the Sun-child, and to hear of all these wonderful things.

Among those who came from distant lands was the Dragon-child. He had returned safe from the wars and was surprised to find his bride changed, although the two step-sisters very much resembled one another. But as the Dragon-child had put a golden tooth in the place of the front tooth of his bride, which was broken in the well, he was able to detect the substitution. Upon a strict examination of his mother, he discovered that the bride had been sent to her stepmother's where, as he supposed, she had been gotten rid of, and was replaced by her stepsister. All his efforts to find his lost bride being in vain, the Dragon-child had come to see the Sun-child and his mother, with the expectation of finding some means for the discovery of his wife. He became a guest in the Sun-child's house, and told his story while they were eating supper. The bride, who was serving at the table, smiled and showed her golden tooth. This caused her to be discovered, and the Sun-child told how she had come and found him. Now as they had partaken of bread together, they had become friends, and agreed to solve the difficulty in a friendly manner. They decided to roast salt meat and make the bride eat it, without letting her drink. Each was to take a pitcher of water, and they all were to go riding in the fields. He whom she should ask for a drink must be her husband. They did so, and took a ride in the fields, the wife accompanying them with her child in her arms. She was thirsty, but not wishing to offend any one of them, she kept silent for a time. Finally she saw that she would faint and must put an end to the perplexed state.

"Sun-child! Sun-child!" she exclaimed.

The Sun-child dismounted and prepared to give her a drink. Thereupon she exclaimed:

"Dragon-child! Dragon-child!"

He also dismounted and prepared to give her a drink.

Turning to the Sun-child, she said:

"Here, take this child whose father you are; but I am the wedded wife of the Dragon-child."

And she drank from the Dragon-child's pitcher, and went home with him.

Thus their trouble ended and they attained their wishes. May all who are afflicted find consolation. Three apples fell from heaven—one for me, one for the storyteller, and one for him who entertained the company.

MIRZA

A king, on suspicion of an attempt to usurp the throne, had put his brother in chains and suspended him between heaven and earth. The King was old, and the day of his death being near, he called his three sons, and advised them not to leave the throne empty, lest their uncle should usurp it and put them to death. After giving the young Princes other important counsel, the old King died. The oldest son, who succeeded his father on the throne, one day went hunting for birds. The youngest brother, whose name was Mirza, remembering their father's advice, immediately leaped up and sat on the throne. In the evening the oldest brother returned and began to scold Mirza, saying:

"How now, rogue! Have you a mind to usurp my throne?"

"No, your majesty," replied Mirza; "I sat on the throne lest our uncle, finding it empty, should usurp it. But if it displeases you I will not do it again."

On the following day the King again went bird-hunting, and the throne was left empty. Suddenly a loud jangling of chains was heard, and lo! The uncle, having broken the fetters, descended from the skies and seated himself on the empty throne. Forthwith he ordered his men to put the three brothers to death, but his officials interceded and begged the King not to kill his nephews, but to banish them from the country. The King consented, and the three brothers were banished.

The lot of the three Princes was now to lead a sad, wandering life in the dreary desert. After a long journey, they came to a ruined mill just at the time when the sun was going down. The elder brothers at once dismounted to spend the night in the ruined mill, but Mirza implored them not to do so, saying:

"Brothers, when our father died he advised us that in case our uncle usurped the throne and banished us, we must take heed not to lodge in a ruined mill, not to camp on a green meadow, and not to resort to the Black Mountain. Come, be advised, lest worse trouble befall."

"Hush, coward!" said the elder brothers, and they prepared to lodge in the mill. The oldest brother said:

"Let us turn the horses out to pasture, and do you two go to bed; I will keep watch all night."

After eating their meal the two younger brothers went to bed, while the oldest began his watch. Mirza shut his eyes and pretended to sleep, peeping, however, through his eyelashes to see what his oldest brother was doing. After watching a while the latter was tired, withdrew and went to bed. By the snoring of his brothers, Mirza understood that they had fallen into sound sleep. He rose, girded on his magic sword, and taking his bow and arrow, began to walk about and to keep watch. In the middle of the night he saw, at a distance, the gleaming of a light, which drew nearer and nearer, and soon, to his terror, he saw a horrible dragon with seven heads, on each of which was an enormous jewel burning like a torch. It approached his brothers and was about to devour them, when Mirza took aim and shot all its seven heads with a single arrow. The monster stretched itself on the ground, hissing and wheezing. The boy drew his magic sword, and cutting the dragon to pieces put the seven jewels in his pocket. He spent the rest of the night watching, and toward morning went to bed and pretended to sleep. On the morrow the oldest brother awoke and nudged Mirza in the side, saying:

"Get up, ho! Have you not slept enough? I was guarding your repose all night long."

All three rose and started upon their journey. They traveled until they came to a green meadow, at the sight of which the two elder brothers dismounted and began to pitch their tents to spend the night, in spite of the entreaties of Mirza, who reminded them of the advice of their father to avoid the green meadow.

"What a coward you are!" exclaimed the second brother. "You need not be so much afraid; I will keep guard tonight," and dismounting, all three pitched their tents on the green meadow. The second brother kept watch till midnight, and then went to bed. Mirza, who was only pretending to sleep, hearing his second brother snore soundly, got up, girded on his magic sword, and taking his bow and arrows, began to keep watch. Soon he saw something approaching the tents. As it drew nearer, he could see that it was a terrible giantess, with one of her lips reaching the skies, and the other sweeping the ground. He at once took ambush in a neighboring trench, and aimed an arrow toward her, saying to himself:

"If she does no harm to my brothers I will not shoot her."

The giantess arrived and was apparently surprised to find three tents, and three horses, but only two men. However, she came to the conclusion that the third human being had been devoured by the wild beasts. She then approached the two sleeping boys and hung a sleep-ring on an ear of each, saying:

"Sleep now, until I send my seven sons to devour you."

Mirza followed her until she came to a large rock, which was the gate of an underground cave. She turned the rock over, and entering the cave, exclaimed to her sons:

"Get up, boys! I have found a good meal for you. Go make your repast on the two human beings, and save a portion for me." Mirza stood at the cave's entrance with his magic sword, and cut off the head of each giant as they came out one by one. Then he entered the cave, and taking hold of the giantess, said:

"Ugly hag! did you dare to send your sons to devour my brothers! Here! share the fate of your younglings." So speaking, he cut her head off too. He came back and found his brothers snoring as before. He took the sleep-rings from their ears, and at daybreak went to bed and feigned sleep. In the morning the second brother jogged Mirza, saying:

"Get up, ho! will you sleep till noon? Have a little mercy on me, who have watched all the night."

They all rose and mounted their horses. That day they came to the Black Mountain, where the two elder brothers desired to camp. Mirza began again to implore them, saying:

"This time, at least, let us follow the advice of our father and not halt on this enchanted ground; let us avoid a third disaster which may perhaps be fatal."

"What a coward you are!" exclaimed his brothers. "What danger was there in lodging in the mill or in camping on the green meadows? As it is your turn to watch tonight, you grumble. Be silent! We will camp here to-night, and you must keep watch."

They pitched their tents, and after a meal, the two elder brothers soon went to bed. Mirza girded on his magic sword, took his bow and arrows, and began his watch. The first part of the night was quiet. After midnight he sat down to take a little rest, and on account of his sleeplessness on the two previous nights, he soon fell asleep. When he opened his eyes it was near daybreak. He rose, and to his great dismay he found the fire was out. It was a sign that he had slept and this would disgrace him. He could not start the fire anew because the flint and steel were in the pockets of the other brothers. He ran to the top of the neighboring hill, whence he saw a light gleaming at a distance. He determined to fetch embers from that light, and make his own fire. On the hilltop he met an old man winding a ball of black thread, while another ball of white thread lay near him.

"Good-day to you, father!" said the boy.

"God's blessing rest upon you!" answered the old man.

"Who are you, and what are these balls?" asked Mirza.

"I am Time," answered the old man; "this black ball signifies the night, which as you see, is near its end. As soon as it finishes, the morning breaks. Then I will roll this white ball, which represents the day, down the hill, and it will go on unwrapping until it is noon. I shall then wrap it again, and finish just when it is evening."

Mirza snatched the black ball from the old man's hand, and rolling it down the hill, unwrapped it, saying:

"Now, father, wrap it up again. I wish this night to be a little longer, for I have much to do."

So saying, he proceeded toward the gleaming light. On arriving he

saw that it came from a cave, with a fireplace over which there was a great cauldron with forty handles. The meat of seven oxen was cooking in the cauldron, around which forty giants were lying asleep. The youth approached the fireplace, seized the cauldron, put it down, taking some embers from under, replaced it and started back on his way. It chanced that one of the giants was watching, and saw what the boy did. As soon as Mirza disappeared, he woke his brothers and told them what the human being had done. All the forty were surprised, and bit their lips upon hearing this marvelous news in regard to a human being, who had displayed a strength surpassing the united force of the forty brothers. At once they decided to make that human hero their partner; so accordingly they ran after him, and overtaking him, proposed to him to be their brother. The boy consented, and they adopted each other as brothers, exchanging promises to go to one another's assistance in case of need. Mirza returned to the camp, and after starting the fire, lay down to take a morning nap. By that time his brothers awakened, and jogged him in the side, saying:

"Get up! we have been watching this night also, and do you still sleep?"

He did not utter a word. They all mounted their horses and went their way until they came to the city of the King of the Black Mountain, and camped in a meadow outside the city. In the middle of the night as Mirza was keeping watch around the camp, he saw giants proceeding toward the palace of the King. Coming nearer he perceived that they were his adopted brothers each carrying a large iron nail as long as a man is high.

"Godspeed!" said Mirza.

"Well met!" answered the giants; "come and help us in our enterprise tonight, and here are three golden apples as a present for you. The King has three daughters whom we have been hunting for seven years, but cannot find. We have prepared these three golden apples for their love, but we will give them to you if you help us. We have made these iron nails to use in climbing the walls."

Mirza's anger began to boil, but he carefully concealed his feeling.

"Very well," he said, at last, "this very night you will attain your desires, but you must obey me."

He walked at their head and the giants followed until

they came to the foot of the palace wall. He took the iron nails, and thrusting them into the wall with his thumb, formed a row of steps by which he could ascend to the top of the wall. He then ordered the giants to mount, and as they went up one by one, he cut off their heads with his magic sword, throwing their bodies into a trench on the other side. Then cutting off the ears of each, he put them in his pocket, and arranged their heads in a row on the top of the wall. After that he jumped over and entered the palace. In the King's bedchamber he saw a golden candlestick burning at the head of the King's bed, and a silver candlestick burning at the foot. Mirza changed the places of the candlesticks, and drank the syrup which was in the golden cup near the King. As he was going out, he saw a dragon coiled around the pillar ready to devour the King. At once he drew his dagger, and stabbed the dragon, nailing it to the pillar. Next he took the

King's dagger from under his pillow and put it in his belt. Then he entered the bedchamber of the three maidens, drank the syrup in their golden cups and placed a golden apple on the pillow of each, thus betrothing the oldest to his oldest brother, the middle one to his middle brother, and the youngest to himself. He also placed on the pillow of the youngest maiden a necklace made of the seven jewels which he had taken by killing the seven-headed dragon in the ruined mill. Then he came back to his tent, and at daybreak went to bed.

When morning came there was a great tumult among the people of the city, who had seen the heads of the forty giants who had been butchered. Informants ran to the King bearing the glad tidings that his forty troublesome enemies had all been killed, that their bodies were lying in the trench and their heads were on the top of the wall. The King, who by that time had discovered what had happened in his palace, was filled with amazement. His peers and subjects came to congratulate him. Upon this the King sent out heralds to proclaim that the one who did all these things, whoever he might be, must present himself. Not only should he become the son-in-law of the King by marrying the most beautiful of the three maidens, but the King would gladly bestow on him any gift which he might ask. Thousands appeared before the King claiming to be the hero, but none could prove it. No man was left in the city who did not make his appearance before the sovereign. Then the King bade his men call the strangers who were camping without the walls. Mirza feigned sickness, and at first did not go. His two brothers feared that they were to be fined for trampling upon the King's ground, but as soon as they were told wherefore they were called, they began to boast that they had done the heroic deed, yet upon trial they also were turned back in shame.

"Is there no one else left?" inquired the King.

"Nobody," answered the attendant, "except a sickly boy lying in the tent of these strangers."

"Bring him hither," ordered the King.

Mirza, seeing the King's attendant about to force him to go, rose, and leaping on the back of his horse, made his appearance before the King. He put before him the ears of the forty giants and told the King how he slew them, how he changed the places of the candlesticks, how he stabbed the dragon, and betrothed the King's daughters to his brothers and to himself. He gave to the King the dagger, and drew out from the pillar his own dagger which neither the King nor his peers had been able to withdraw. The King sprang from his throne and kissed Mirza on the forehead, exclaiming:

"May Heaven bless you, worthy hero! You are my beloved son-in-law, and after my death my throne is yours."

His brothers bowed down before Mirza, saying:

"Pardon our harshness; hereafter you are our elder brother and we are your subordinates."

After that there was a great wedding festival for forty days and forty nights, and the three maidens were given in marriage to the three brothers. At the nuptials, however, the brides said to the bridegrooms:

"We are not for you, such frail men as you are. Do you think killing forty dwarfish giants a heroic act? Not so. We have our lover, upon whose breast roses and lilies grow. If you are men of valor, go fight the Roaring Giant, our lover; if you can overcome him we are yours, but not until you do so."

On the following morning, Mirza advised his brothers to keep silent and not reveal their secret, lest they should be the laughing-stock of the people. He took leave of the King, saying that he had an important work to do, and would be absent for two months. He started, and after a long journey came to a white castle. A maiden as beautiful as the moon was sitting in the window working with her needle. Seeing the boy, she said to him:

"Human being, neither the snake on its belly, nor the bird with its wing could come here! How could you venture to come?"

"Your love brought me hither, fair maiden," answered the boy.

"Here is food for you," said the maiden, letting down from the window a basket; "eat, and go your way. This castle belongs to the White Giant. Go away before he comes, lest he devour you."

"Who are you, fair maiden? Who has brought you hither?" inquired the boy.

"My father is the King of India. We were three sisters,

but the White Giant, the Red Giant, and the Black Giant stole us and brought us into this lonely country. It has been seven years since I have seen a human being."

Mirza asked if she knew where the Roaring Giant lived.

"You must pass the lands of the Red Giant and the Black Giant before you arrive," said the maiden.

"Farewell!" said Mirza.

"Farewell!" said the fair maiden, sighing

Mirza continued on his way. Toward evening he saw the White Giant returning from hunting. He detected his presence by the human smell, and seeing Mirza, exclaimed:

"What luck! I have not tasted human flesh for a long time;" and he assailed Mirza, to devour him.

"Halt!" exclaimed the boy, preparing his bow and arrow. "I shall prove a hard nut for you to crack. My name is Mirza. I have so far butchered forty-seven giants; you are the forty-eighth."

He shot his arrow, which passed through the giant's heart and nailed him to the ground. Drawing his magic sword, he cut off his head, and thrusting it on his sword's point took it to the white castle and called to the maiden:

"Fair Princess, here is the head of the White Giant, whom I have sacrificed to your love."

The maiden seeing it from the window, ran wild with joy. At once she opened the door of the castle, saying:

"Enter, and may Heaven bless you, who came to deliver me from my bondage!"

The boy entered, and that night lodged in the castle. On the morning, when departing, he put on the maiden's finger a ring, saying:

"Now you are the betrothed of my oldest brother. After

fighting the other giants I will come back and carry you with me."

And he took leave of her. After a long journey he came to a black castle with a beautiful maiden sitting in the window, who gave him refreshment as the former had done. Leaving her, he met the Black Giant, and killing him as he had the former one, brought his head to the maiden. He spent the night there, and on the following morning, putting a ring on the finger of the maiden, betrothed her to his second brother. Another long journey brought him to a red castle. A maiden as beautiful as the sun was sitting in the window and working with her needle. The boy at first glance fell in love with her. She also had fallen in love with him at first sight, and said to him:

"Human being, for Heaven's sake, beware of the Red Giant!"

"I have come on purpose to fight with him, fair creature," answered the boy. "I have already killed the White Giant and the Black Giant and freed your sisters."

"But the Red Giant is a sorcerer," said the maiden, "and when brought to bay, changes himself into a mound of earth, with a hole at the top, whence he pours out smoke and flames, and devours everyone who ventures to go near."

He had hardly departed from the maiden, when lo! the Red Giant appeared, brandishing his terrible mace.

"Aha!" exclaimed the Giant, seeing the boy, "a delicious morsel indeed is this which has come to me of its own free will."

"Nay, come, let us fight," said the boy, "and see who shall be the morsel, I or you!" and he prepared his bow and arrow.

"Dwarfish human being!" exclaimed the giant, "how can

you oppose me?"

Saying this, he threw his mace at the boy, who took hold of it, exclaiming:

"I have killed forty-nine giants, your White and Black brothers included. Mirza is my name; do you think you will escape from my hand?"

When the giant heard that this was Mirza, the terror of the giants, he was so frightened that he at once changed himself into a red mound with smoke and flames shooting out from the hole in its top. Immediately the boy jumped on the mound, drew his magic sword and thrusting it into the smoking hole, began quickly to stir it until the heart and intestines of the Giant were cut to pieces and were thrown out of the orifice. The youth then jumped down, and lo! the mound fell and was ruined. Mirza then went back to the red castle and called to the maiden.

"Fair Princess," he said, showing her his sword dyed with blood and the pieces of the giant's heart and intestines still clinging to it, "I have sacrificed the Red Giant to your love."

The maiden was almost wild with joy. She opened the door, and embracing Mirza's feet, exclaimed:

"Hero! you have saved me; I owe you my life and all my being. I am still a virgin, and though unworthy to be your wife, for Heaven's sake accept me as your handmaid!"

"Nay, fair maiden, you are my love, you are my betrothed if you do love me," said the boy, putting a ring on her finger.

Then the boy asked her concerning the place where lived the Roaring Giant.

"Be advised, do not go," said the maiden. "The Roaring Giant is a cruel tyrant; you will not come back alive; do not go. He is vulnerable only by his own bow and arrows, and who shall give them to you that you may shoot him with them? It is impossible. For the sake of the love you bear to me, do not go, or take me with you that I may die with you," and the maiden began to sob.

"Nay, love, do not cry," said the boy, "I must go at any risk."

And he started. After a long journey he came to a magnificent castle decorated with gold and jewels. It was the castle of the Roaring Giant. It was toward evening when the boy arrived. At once he took the shape of a servant, sprinkled water about the palace, swept all clean, and hid himself behind the trees and bushes. Soon a noise like that of thunder was heard, from the distant mountains. It was the Roaring Giant who was coming from fowling. Every bird, every beast of the forest hid itself on hearing the noise of the giant. Mirza's hair stood on end, and he felt what a terrible task it was which he had undertaken. The giant, seeing the courtyard round the palace swept and cleaned was pleased, and soliloquized to himself:

"This must be the work of a human being; I must find him out; it would be pleasant to have a human servant." And he exclaimed:

"Where are you, human being? Who are you? Come out from your hiding place. I will not hurt you, but give you what you desire."

Mirza leaped out from his place of concealment, and stood before the Roaring Giant, saying in a humble voice:

"My lord, I have lost my companions and gone astray. Heaven was kind enough to guide me until I came to your door. Will you accept me as your servant?"

The giant accepted him, and the boy served so diligently and devotedly that the giant was greatly pleased, and held him in high esteem. One day the giant and the boy entered the flower garden. Roses, violets and other flowers of every color and perfume grew there luxuriously. Nightingales, birds of paradise, and all kinds of birds and beasts of the forest were there. In the middle of the orchard a fountain gushed out its crystal waters, and formed a pond amid overhanging verdure. It was, throughout, a paradise.

"Bring those flower pots and put them around this pond," said the giant to the boy. "Bring here all kinds of delicious foods, which you have prepared. Every day this week we shall have company, and we must prepare for them."

The boy made the necessary preparations meditating to himself that the expected guests were no doubt the three sisters, the wives of himself and his brothers. Near the pond there was a tree on which the giant had hung his bow and arrows. The boy took them down.

"Halloo! what are you doing?" exclaimed the giant.

"Master, I wish to take the cloth and clean them," answered the boy.

Soon the arrow fell down.

"Bring it to me," said the giant, and putting the arrow in the bow handed it over to the boy. He took it and went backward as if to hang it up. He had scarcely come to the tree, when he turned to the giant and took aim at his heart.

"Alas!" exclaimed the giant.

"Nay, I have come expressly to take your life," said Mirza. "I am Mirza. I have killed fifty giants; you are the fifty-first."

Whiz! and the arrow was flung and pierced the Roaring Giant through the heart and nailed him to the ground. He uttered his last roar, and then lay dead as a stone. The boy thereupon hid himself behind a tree near the pond to see what might happen.

Soon three turtledoves came from the sky flapping their wings and perched gently on the border of the pond. At once they dove into the water and were changed into three maidens. The boy saw that they were his own wife and the wives of his brothers. He kept silent and did not stir. The maidens, putting on the human dresses which they had brought with them, went to embrace the Roaring Giant, who they supposed was asleep. But seeing him nailed to the ground with an arrow through his heart and dead, they were horror-stricken. They ran back to the pond, and undressing themselves, leaped into the water. Just at that time, Mirza came up and stood on the brink of the pond.

"For shame!" he exclaimed. "How now! did you see your lover? Did you enjoy the roses and the lilies growing on his breast?"

They were horror-stricken and mute, hiding their faces with their hands. Mirza cut pieces from the skirts of their dresses, and let them go. They were turned to turtledoves, and flew away with drooping wings. Thereupon Mirza entering the palace of the Roaring Giant, gathered all the riches and loaded them on forty camels. He then went and took the three Princesses whom he had betrothed to himself and his brothers, also the wealth of the Red, Black and White giants. Then he drove back and came again to the city of the King of the Black Mountain. The King hearing that Mirza had come, bringing inestimable wealth, hastened to meet him at the city gate, all his noblemen and peers accompanying him. As soon as they met, Mirza said to the King:

"I cannot talk with you until you convoke a meeting of all the noblemen and wise men of your realm to try your three daughters."

"What!" said the King, "is it not a shame to bring maidens to trial?"

"Nay," said the boy, "your daughters are false, and

shameless; they must be tried and punished as an example to the womanhood of the realm. If you do not call a meeting as I have requested, I will leave you and go elsewhere."

Now the King loved Mirza as his very life, and could not part with him. So he gave the order and all the peers and wise men of his realm were summoned to a parliament. The three maidens were brought before the court. Mirza recited his adventures, and placed before the court the pieces which he had cut from the dresses of the maidens. On being put in their respective places they fitted. Thus everything being proved, the maidens could not deny it. The court gave its decision, which the King sanctioned. Thereupon the three daughters of the King were bound by their hair to the tails of three wild horses, which were whipped up and carried them away to the wilderness, dashing them from stone to stone until they were cut into pieces.

Then the King adopted the three Princesses whom Mirza had brought with him. A wedding festival for forty days and nights was celebrated, and the three maidens were given in marriage to the three brothers.

Three apples fell from heaven—one for me, one for the story-teller, and one for him who entertained the company.

THE MAGIC RING

Long ago there was an old woman who had a son, whom she always advised not to cause injury to anyone, and not to torture or kill any animal or beast, no matter how despised it might be. They were very poor. The boy went to the forest every day, and brought a bundle of wood on his back. He sold it for twopence and bought bread for his aged mother and himself. One day he saw that the village boys were torturing a kitten and taking pleasure in its cries.

"Why do you torture the poor animal?" said the boy to the boys; "Let it go."

"Give us your pennies, and we will let it go," said the boys.

He at once gave them the twopence which he had earned that day by selling his wood, and took the kitten home with him. Both mother and son went to bed hungry that night. On the following day he took the kitten with him to the forest, and that evening the bundle of wood was sold for four coins. He paid two coins for bread, and putting the other two coins in his pocket was returning home, when he met the village boys who were this time torturing a mouse. The boy gave his two coins to the boys, and took the mouse home with him. On the third day he saved a whelp of a dog and brought it home. On the fourth day he saved a little snake, and putting it in a jug, kept it at home. On the following day he took all the animals and went to the forest to cut wood. At noon he sat at a fountain to eat his lunch, and gave a share of it to the animals. He took the snake out of the jug and let it go, but the reptile would not leave him. He then gave it a piece of bread. As soon as it bit the bread, lo! It was changed into a pretty boy, and said to the boy:

"I am the son of the King of India; magicians stole me and changed me into a snake. The enchantment was such that the moment a human being gave me bread to eat with his own hand, I should again change into a boy. I escaped from the hands of the magicians, and came to the village for the purpose of biting a piece of bread from a human hand, but the village urchins found me and were about to kill me when you saved me. I owe you my life and my freedom from the magician's spell. Now let me advise you. When I go home to my father he will be so happy to see me that he will wish to reward you with the most precious things in his kingdom. But when he asks you to demand something from him, be careful and request only the ring that he has on his finger. It is a magic ring, and the moment you turn its jewel upside-down two genii will wait on you to do your will, and will bring for you anything that you may desire."

The boy accompanied the boy to the court of the King of India, who was so glad at the sight of his child that he was almost beside himself with joy. The boy told his father all that had happened, and presented the boy as the deliverer of his life.

"Ask of me what you will," said the King to the boy, "you have saved the heir apparent, and I will give you whatever you demand, even to the half of my kingdom."

"Long live the King!" said the boy. "I desire only the ring on your finger."

"A plague upon him who advised you!" said the King; "you have demanded the costliest thing I have. But as I have promised I must give it to you."

So saying he gave the ring to the boy, and ordered his

saddlebags to be filled with gold. The boy came back to his aged mother and told her what had happened.

"Well then, son," said the old woman, "let me go and ask our King to give you his daughter in marriage."

The boy consented, and the old woman, after buying for herself a new dress and adorning herself as best she could, went to the court.

"What do you want?" said the King.

"Long live the King!" said the old woman. "I have come to ask you by God's order, to give your daughter in marriage to my son."

"Good," said the King; "but has your son the equivalent of the dower that I can give to my daughter?"

"Certainly he has," answered the woman, "how much do you want him to have?"

"He must have a treasure full of gold like mine, and a magnificent palace like mine. The road between my palace and his must be covered with a single soft rug, and on both sides shady trees must grow, and under them horsemen ride from one end to the other on horses all milky white. If he can procure these I will give him my daughter in marriage; if not, I will not."

The old woman returned and told the boy what the King had said. The boy turned the jewel of the ring, and lo! two genii presented themselves with their hands folded upon their breasts, saying:

"Tell us your will, and we will do it immediately."

The boy ordered them to prepare all that the King had demanded. Everything was ready in one night. On the following day the King was greatly pleased with the palace and everything in it, and gave his daughter in marriage. There they lived in happiness until the death of the old woman.

But there was a Jew who had heard of the magic ring, and he was anxious to get it. He took on the shape of a peddler, and came to the palace at a time when the boy had gone hunting, and there was no one there besides the Princess. She opened the door to look at the goods of the peddler.

"I peddle nice goods for ladies," said the clever Jew; "and in order to give ladies facility, I do not care to sell them for money, but exchange for old jewellery, such as rings and the like. Any lady will have some old rings which she can give in return for beautiful goods."

"Let me see if we have rings at home which I can give you for your goods," said the Princess.

She went in, and came back with the magic ring, saying:

"Here, I have found this among my husband's things; I think it will do for you."

The Jew gave some rubbish in exchange for the precious ring. As soon as he put it on his finger, he turned the jewel, and lo! The two genii stood before him, ready to do his commands.

"I wish you to take this palace, with me in it, and carry it to the Island of the Seven Seas, and I wish you to throw the former owner into the unfathomable sea." He had hardly finished his words when the palace, with the Princess and the Jew, was transported to the Island of the Seven Seas. Then the genii seized the boy, and were about to throw him into the bottomless sea, when they took pity on him, he being their former master, and left him in a wilderness on the shore. This was a dreadful change for the youth. He travelled a long way, and at length came to the hut of a fisherman, who accepted him as an apprentice.

But let us return to the animals. The dog, the cat and the mouse, seeing what misfortune had come to their master, decided to go to the Island of the Seven Seas, and getting the ring from the Jew, take it to their master, whom they knew by instinct to have become the apprentice of a fisherman. They immediately started and soon came to the sea. The dog entered the water, the cat took her seat on his neck, while the mouse rode on the cat's back. The dog began to swim, and proved to be an expert in the art.

"We hope our weight will not cause you to sink brother dog," said the cat and the mouse.

"Pshaw!" said the dog, proudly, "you are as light as a feather, and speak of sinking me! Nay, be careful not to be blown away from my back by the wind of my respiration."

And out of his mouth he hung his long tongue. So swimming, at last they came to the Island of the Seven Seas, where they saw their master's palace. It was night. The dog stood at the bottom of the wall while the cat with the mouse on her back climbed up until they came to the window. But as it was closed it was now the turn of the mouse to do his part. He gnawed the board with his fine teeth and opened a hole large enough for himself to go through. Entering, he looked everywhere for the ring, but it could not be found. The Jew was asleep.

"Look at the Jew's fingers," whispered the cat from without.

But it was not there

"Look in his mouth," whispered the cat.

The mouse made a careful examination, and lo! The ring was in the Jew's mouth. But how to get it? The mouse saw that the Jew had put his snuffbox near his bed. He first ran to the cellar, and soaked his tail in vinegar; then coming back he thrust it into the snuffbox. He repeated this several times, until his tail was well stiffened with a coating of vinegar and snuff. He went then to the sleeping Jew, and perching upon his beard thrust his tail into his nostril as far as it could go.

This caused the Jew to sneeze with all his might, and lo! The ring was flung from his mouth. The mouse uttered a shriek of joy, and snatching the ring from the floor, in the twinkling of an eye disappeared through the hole. The Jew immediately arose, and lighting a candle began to search for the ring. Not finding it, he thought to look for it in the morning, and again went to bed. The mouse and the cat descended the wall to their big-mouthed friend, who was looking at them wistfully. The dog again entered the water, the cat took her place on his back, and the mouse rested on the cat's back. They decided that the ring should be in the cat's mouth. This time they began to swim toward the opposite shore of the sea, where the boy was serving the fisherman. They crossed the Seven Seas and approached the shore safely. As soon as they saw the land and their master's hut, the dog said to his companions:

"I am swimming for you, but you have the ring. You will give it to master, who will praise you; while I, who have worked the hardest, will not receive any credit. Not so; you must put the ring in my mouth before we reach the land."

"Brother dog," said the cat, "now you are tired and see how you keep your mouth open all the time and stretch your tongue out. If we put the ring in your mouth, we are afraid you will drop it into the sea. But as soon as we reach the land, we will give the ring to you, that you may give it to master."

"No," said the dog, "you must give it now, or else I will drop you into the sea."

He began to shake them, threatening to drown them. The cat, therefore, was obliged to place the ring in the dog's mouth. But he could not keep his mouth shut a single minute. He opened his mouth, stretched his tongue, began to pant, and lo! The ring fell into the sea. They came ashore, but all in great excitement. The mouse and the cat began to beat the dog, who thrust his tail between his hind legs as if to acknowledge his fault, but had to defend himself against the sharp paws of the cat and the fine teeth of the mouse. Quarrelling and howling and rolling upon the sand, they came to the fisherman's hut. The boy, with his natural kindness to animals, came out to separate the fighters, and lo! They were his own friends. Seeing the boy, all three paid him their respects, but again began to fight one another, this time more severely. The youth, seeing that it was impossible to leave them in this way, provided three ropes, and bound them separately. He gave them food and drink, and tried to calm their anger. On the following day he drew out a net full of fishes, and sat down to prepare them for market. Among them was a large fish. As soon as the boy seized it, there was excitement among the animals. The dog barked, the cat mewed, and the mouse shrieked, and all three tried to cut their ropes. The boy had hardly cut the fish open when the mouse, having gnawed its rope, ran and plunged into the belly of the fish, and in the twinkling of an eye came out with the magic ring in its mouth, for the fish had swallowed the ring. The mouse jumped upon his master's lap and presented the ring, at sight of which the boy understood why the animals were troubled. He untied them, and kissing the three, expressed his gratitude for their brave enterprise. Then he turned the jewel, and lo! The two genii presented themselves.

"I want my palace to be restored to its place, myself to be placed in it again, and the Jew to be thrown into the bottomless sea," said the boy.

He had barely finished his sentence when he found himself and his animal friends in his palace once more, and near him was his wife. The Jew was cast into the bottomless sea, where he is sinking everlastingly but never reaches the bottom. Thus the wicked one was punished and the virtuous one attained his wishes. May Heaven grant that you may all be virtuous and attain your wishes!

Three apples fell from heaven—one for me, one for the story-teller, and one for the man who entertained the company.

THE TWINS

In the springtime a certain King pitched his tent in a flowery meadow tract, among shady trees and near a gurgling brook. There came from the village three sisters, maidens of marriageable age, to gather flowers and edible vegetables. At noon they sat down on the bank of the crystal brook, not far from the royal tent, and began to prattle.

"If the King takes me in marriage for his eldest son," said the oldest maiden, "I will weave for him a tent so big that it will accommodate all his army, and yet one-half of it will be empty."

"If the King takes me in marriage for his second son," said the second maiden, "I will weave for him a rug so big that it will accommodate all his court and the people of his realm, and yet half of it will be left empty."

"I will not brag," said the youngest sister; "but if the King takes me in marriage for his youngest son, and if it pleases Heaven, I will give birth to twins—a silver-haired boy and a golden-haired girl."

The two older maidens laughed at their young sister and ridiculed her. The King, who was listening to the talk of the maidens from behind the tapestry, was pleased with them and gave all three in marriage to his three sons. One day he asked of the oldest sister:

"Where is the tent which you were going to weave?"

"It was only vain prattle we sisters were indulging in," she said.

"Where is your rug?" inquired the King of the second sister.

"It was merely idle talk," she replied.

"And where are your twins?" asked he of the youngest sister.

"If it pleases Heaven I will bear them in the fullness of time," she replied.

The older sisters became very envious of their younger sister and they vowed to be revenged, for now the love and caresses of the whole court seemed to be bestowed upon her. One night there came to the arms of the youngest sister the promised silver-haired boy and golden-haired girl. The envious sisters immediately took the babies away and put them into a chest that they threw into the river. Bringing a pair of puppies, they placed them by the bedside of the young mother. Then they went to the young Prince and informed him that his beloved wife was mother to the two puppies. The young Prince was horror-stricken. The King was mad with rage. He ordered his servants to wrap the young woman in a camel's hide and put her in the corner by the palace door, so that every one who entered the palace might spit in her face, for her base conduct in thus bringing shame upon those who had loved and favored her. The King's order was at once put into execution.

It so happened that there was an old man and his wife living in a hut on the banks of the river on the outskirts of the city. The old man used to cast his nets into the river every day and catch two fish, one for himself and one for his wife. On that day he threw his net for fish, and lo! a chest was drawn out. He took it to his hut where he and his wife opening it saw that there was in it a pair of pretty babies. The silver-haired boy had put his thumb into the mouth of the golden-haired girl, and the girl had put her thumb into the mouth of the boy. So they were sucking one another's thumbs and were not crying at all. The aged couple looked upon them with great joy and said:

"Thank Heaven! We were till now without offspring, and lo! Heaven has now granted us twins."

The old lady washed the babies, and lo! Gold and silver fell down from their hair. She said to her husband—

"Now, husband, get up and take this gold and silver to the mart and buy for us a cow that we may feed the babies with milk."

The old man went, and with that silver and gold bought not only a cow, but a great many other things necessary for the twins, who were brought up with great care and kindness, although in an obscure hut. The children grew rapidly and became a great comfort to the aged couple. The boy grew to be a brave boy and became a hunter, and the girl grew to be a beautiful, intelligent maiden. The aged couple, following the course of the world, died when the children were quite young. The girl had only once heard from the old woman that they were fished from the river in a chest, and that the despised woman in the King's palace door was their mother, whom the King's two daughters-in-law had put in that position by falsehood. After the death of their benefactors, the sister and brother continued to live in the hut. The boy went hunting, and the maiden used to visit the court, for the purpose of seeing their mother; but, following the advice of her deceased godmother, she did not let herself be known, lest mischief should befall herself and her brother. She learned, however, all that was going on in the royal palace. One day the boy hunted for an antelope and found a fine one, which he secured.

"This is worthy of the King," said the boy, and took it to the palace. The King was very much pleased. On another day he shot a lion, whose skin he took to the King, who said to him:

"Good for you, my little hunter! Come to-morrow to the palace again; I will praise you before my men."

The boy came home and told his sister that he was invited to the palace by the King.

"Good!" said the maiden; "take this bouquet with you. When you enter the King's palace you will see there, in a corner, a woman wrapped in the hide of a camel, and buried in the dust up to her waist. All who enter the door spit in her face; for my sake, do throw this bunch of roses to her as you pass by her."

"All right," said the boy; and on the following day, as he was entering the palace, he threw the bunch of roses to the despised woman. He then entered the King's apartment, where both the King and the courtiers were very much pleased with him. His manly bearing and intelligent conversation were the subject of general admiration. But the King's two daughters-in-law were very much displeased with the little hunter, who threw a bunch of roses to their disgraced sister instead of spitting at her. They thought there was something at the bottom of the boy's conduct, and said to one another:

"Let us find out some means of getting rid of this urchin, lest our secret should leak out."

As they had great influence with the King and the court, they went to the King and said:

"Long live the King! You see that this boy is an expert hunter; he has brought you a lion's hide; but it shall be useless as long as there is only one. Send him to bring a dozen more lions' skins with which to adorn the new palace."

The King liked this suggestion and sent the boy to bring

him a dozen lions' skins. The boy came home and told his sister, who said to him:

"Brother, when our godmother died she told me that we had an aunt living somewhere among the rocks of yonder Black Mountains. In case some difficult task was imposed upon us by the court we might go to our aunt, who would always be glad to help us. So you had better go to her; she will show you how to hunt twelve lions."

The boy started towards the Black Mountains. There, in a deep cavern, he saw an old fairy woman sitting. He ran to her and at once kissed her hand.

"Halloo!" exclaimed the old lady, "is it you, silver-haired twin?"

"Yes, auntie, it is me," answered the boy.

"And how does your golden-haired sister thrive?" the fairy woman asked.

"She humbly kisses both of your hands, auntie," said the boy.

"And what have you come for, my boy?" inquired the fairy lady.

"The King wants from me a dozen lions' skins," answered the boy.

"Well then, come and hide you under my apron till your forty cousins come," said the old woman, hiding the boy in the folds of her skirts.

Soon the forty fairies, the sons of the old lady, came, and smelling the boy, exclaimed:

"How now, mother! Have you prepared for us a meal of human meat today?"

"No, sons," answered the lady, "unless you are so cruel as to eat your own human cousin."

"Where is he, mother?" inquired the forty, "we will not hurt him, but talk to him."

The boy came out from under the apron of his fairy aunt.

The forty brothers were very much pleased with him and kissed him by turns. Then they asked him about his errand, and when the boy told them, they said:

"That is nothing, cousin, we will give you twelve lions' skins which we are now using as quilts and replace them with new ones tomorrow."

They gave the boy the lions' skins to carry to the King, also a tent as a present to his golden-haired sister. The boy came home, and giving the tent to his sister, took the skins to the King, who was highly pleased with them. But the two women were more uneasy now than ever, and asked the King to send the boy to bring seven pairs of elephants' tusks, in order to decorate the new palace with ivory. The King, not knowing that the intention of the wicked women was to destroy the youth, sent him to bring the ivory. The boy went again to his fairy cousins and told his errand.

"Cousin," said the forty brothers, "we can bring you seven pairs of elephants' tusks, but you must bring us a saw, and seven horse-loads of seven-year-old wine."

The boy went back to the city, and getting the saw and seven skinfuls of old wine, loaded them on seven horses and brought them to the fairies, who took them to the pool which was the elephants' watering-place. They emptied the water from the pool and filled it with wine. At night the elephants came to drink, and not knowing that it was wine, they soon were drunken and fell down senseless. Thereupon the fairies cut off their tusks and brought them to the boy. Besides this they gave him also a rug as a present for the golden-haired maiden. The boy came home, and giving the rug to his sister, he took the ivory to the King, who was very much pleased with it. But the King's two daughters-in-law were very angry at the boy's success, and went again to the King, saying:

"Long live the King! The new palace is very nicely decorated with lions' skins and ivory, but it has one deficiency, and that is a beautiful mistress to dwell in it. The King of India's daughter must live there. Her beauty is unequalled in the world. And as your youngest son is without a wife, she will be his wife. Send the little hunter to bring her."

The King was persuaded and sent the boy on the errand. The youth again went to his fairy cousins, who kidnaped and brought the daughter of the King of India safely, and gave her to the boy. They gave to him also a table, which was served by itself, as a present. He fell in love with the maiden at first sight; she also fell in love with the boy. But as he had promised to take her to the King, he did so. The King ordered him to take the maiden to the new palace, and invited the boy who was the hero of so many great deeds to a private banquet at the palace. The two wicked women, seeing that they could not destroy the boy by sending him on difficult errands, were mad with anger. The boy went home and told his sister that the King had invited him for the following day.

"Brother," said the maiden, "when you go to-morrow to the King's palace, take your hound with you. Let it go before you, and you step only wherever it has stepped. And when you eat, first give your dog to eat of the meat. If you see it has not hurt him, you may eat of the meat; but if he dies, be careful not to eat, lest you die also."

On the following day the boy did as the maiden had advised him and sent the dog before him. Just under the threshold of the door there was a deep pit dug which was discovered by the dog's walking before him, and he avoided it. Entering in, he cast the bouquet which his sister had given him to the woman in the dust. And when he was called to the table he gave a piece of the food to the dog, and lo! it died at once. Thereupon he withdrew, saying:

"I am not hungry to-day. I had my meal before I came."

He refused to touch any of the food, in spite of the polite entreaties of the King's two daughters-in-law. Then in his interview with the King he asked his majesty to accept his invitation and come to his humble home for dinner, with all the court. The King, who by this time had become very much fascinated with the appearance of the youth, accepted his invitation. In the evening the boy came home and told his sister what had happened.

"Do you know who digged the pit under the threshold?" asked the maiden.

"Who?" said the boy.

"The King's two daughters-in-law," said the maiden, "in order that you might fall into it and be killed."

"But they were so friendly and polite," said the boy.

"And do you know why your dog died?" inquired the maiden.

"Why?" said the boy.

"The King's two daughters-in-law had poisoned the food, in order to kill you," said the maiden.

"Strange!" exclaimed the boy, "what have I done to them?"

"And do you know who the woman is who is buried in the dust and to whom you have given bunches of roses while all others spat at her?" asked the maiden.

"Oh! her lot is most pitiful; for Heaven's sake tell me who she is," said the boy.

"She is our mother, the one who gave us our existence," said she.

"How! how!" exclaimed the boy, impatiently.

The maiden told him everything. She also told him that it was their cruel aunts who, wanting to destroy him, had persuaded the King to send him on dangerous errands. Then sister and brother planned how to entertain the King on the following day. They at first pitched the tent sent by the fairies, and lo! it was so large that a whole kingdom could be entertained in it. Then they stretched the rug, and lo! it was as large as the tent. Then they put in the middle of it the wishing-table, which served as much and as many kinds of food as one desires. On the following day the King with all the court and the army came, and seeing the tent the King said to himself:

"Aha! this is the tent that my oldest daughter-in-law would weave."

Entering in, he saw the immense rug, and he said to himself:

"This is the rug which my second daughter-in-law was boasting about."

All his army was entertained and there was still room for as many more people. The King fell into deep meditation and thought there must be something at the bottom of it all. The foods served from the wishing-table were so various and delicious that the King was very much pleased, and at the end of the banquet, while all the crowd was listening, he said to the twins:

"Ask of me whatever you want, and I will give it to you, even to the half of my kingdom."

"Is there anything more precious than father and mother?" said the twins; "mighty King, give us our father and mother."

"Although I am a King," said the King, "do not forget that I am human. Is it possible that a human being should give you your lost parents?"

"How is it," said the twins, "that you believe that a human being can give birth to dogs, and you do not believe a human being to be able to restore lost parents? If one is true, the other also must be true."

A thunderbolt suddenly falling from the sky would not have frightened the King's two daughters-in-law as much as did these words.

"What do you mean?" said the King, with a trembling voice.

The twins told him their story, at the end of which the boy took off his cap, displaying his silver hair; and the maiden took off her head-dress, letting fall her rich golden locks. Thereupon the King embraced his grandchildren, weeping loudly because of great joy. Then they embraced the Prince, their father, and their dear, wronged mother, who was immediately released from her disgraceful punishment. The King at once ordered the furnace to be heated to seven times the usual heat, and the two wicked women were thrown into the fire. Then a wedding was celebrated for forty days and nights and the boy was married to the daughter of the King of India, whom he had brought to the palace.

Thus Heaven rewarded the good and punished the evil.

Three apples fell from heaven—one for me, one for the story-teller, and one for him who entertained the company.

BEDIK AND THE INVULNERABLE GIANT

Many years ago there was a King who had seven sons. As soon as each one of the princes was of age his father sent him on an expedition, that he might display his bravery and marry the maiden whom he preferred. Thus six of the princes acquired wives, but Heaven only knows whether they displayed real bravery or not. It was now the turn of the seventh son, whose name was Bedik[1]. His father gave him a horse of lightning, a magic sword and a bow-and-arrow, saying:

"Go, my son, and may Heaven grant you good luck."

Bedik started and travelled through the length and breadth of the world, visiting the land of darkness, the land of light, the land of fairies, the land of giants. He did battle with men, beasts, genii, and all kinds of creatures which he encountered on the way, and overcame them all, but in his wars he lost all his servants and his wealth. He was alone, one day, when he came to a magnificent castle built of marble, decorated with gold and jewels and surrounded with orchards and flower gardens. He walked about the building and gazed everywhere, but could see no human being, man or woman. He waited all the day, concealed behind some bushes. Toward evening there came a Giant covered all over with armor, brandishing his bow and arrows, which were of heavy steel. When he walked the earth trembled. When he came near the castle, becoming aware of the presence of a human being, he exclaimed:

"Aha! I smell a human being. I go a-hunting to the mountains, and lo! The prey has come to my home. Ho! human

1 Bedik is an Armenian male given name meaning "little prince".

being, disclose yourself; else I will make a morsel of you."

The boy was looking at the Giant from his place of concealment. He was the strangest creature that he had ever seen; neither a sword nor an arrow could pierce him. Nevertheless he decided to face him, and coming out from behind the bushes, he stood before him.

"Who are you?" asked the Giant. "The bird with its wing, and the snake on its belly could not approach this castle of mine; and how could you venture to come? Have you not heard of the fame of the Invulnerable Giant?"

"I have," said the boy bravely, "and my name is no less famous than yours; I am Bedik; I have traveled all over the world, and having heard of you, I came to measure swords with you."

The Giant gazed at the boy for a moment and suddenly sneezed. The burst of air through his nostrils caused the boy to leap ten rods away.

"Halloo!" exclaimed the Giant, laughing, "you do not seem to be very well able to fight me, do you? Nay, come here again; do not be afraid, I will not hurt you. I have heard about you; you are a brave little fellow. But you see you can do no harm to me, because I am invulnerable. Come, be my servant, for I need a skillful human servant, and I do not think I can find a better one than you. Bring your sword and bow and arrows. You see they are not available to pierce me; we may need them for hunting and other purposes."

The boy consented, and they lived together for a time. One day the Giant said to the youth:

"You see I am immortal, but I have an anxiety which gnaws my heart day and night. The King of the East has a daughter, and there is no beauty like hers under the sun. I have made seven expeditions to carry her away, but so far have not succeeded. If you can bring her here I will bestow upon you a kingly reward."

"I will bring her for you," said the boy.

"But do you promise it upon your soul?" said the Giant.

"I do," answered the boy, and at once started on the expedition.

After a long journey he came to the city of the King of the East, changed his clothes, took the shape of a farmer boy, and became the apprentice of the King's gardener. He saw the King's daughter sitting in her window and working with her needle. She was so beautiful that she seemed to say to the sun, "Sun, you need not shine, since I am shining." The boy fell in love with her and began to curse the hour when he made the solemn promise to convey her to the Giant. One day, taking advantage of the absence of his master, the boy stripped off his humble clothes, and putting on his princely garments, mounted his horse of lightning and rode in the King's garden. The maiden was looking from her window and saw him. She had never seen a young man so perfect, and she fell in love with him. On the following day she sent two of her maids to the youth, informing him of her love. The boy sent her word who he was, how he had heard of her wondrous beauty, and now he was waiting to do anything that she might order. The city was surrounded by high walls, through fear of the Invulnerable Giant, who assaulted it every year with the intention of carrying off the maiden; but the people of the city, being brave fighters, would not let the maiden be borne away. So the boy had a hard task to perform. One day the girl sent to him, through her maids, the following message:

"Tomorrow is the feast of the Navasard[2], when all the maidens of the city go out for recreation and merriment, but I am not allowed to go forth because it is the day when the Invulnerable Giant makes his annual assault to seize me. I will, however, go to the garden by the riverside, which is surrounded by high walls; there I will wait for you to see you display your bravery."

Having received this message, on the next day the youth put on his princely garments, girded his magic sword, and taking his bow and arrows, mounted his horse of lightning. Once or twice he coursed the steed near the garden wall, until it began to gallop as fast as if it had wings. One stroke of the whip, and lo! it jumped over the wall like an eagle, and instantly the horse and its rider alighted in the middle of the garden. In the twinkling of an eye the boy put his arm around the maiden's waist, and placing her behind him on the saddle, gave another stroke of the whip, which made the horse leap over the garden wall, and in a second they were on safe ground outside the city galloping like a flash of lightning. The maids in attendance were horror-stricken, thinking that it was a hurricane that had taken their boy from them. It was a long time before they understood what had taken place; then they informed the King, who sent out his bravest horsemen in pursuit of the fugitives. But it was too late. The couple on the back of the horse of lightning passed over the mountains and valleys until they came to the border of the deep river. A stroke of the whip and the steed swam the deep waters and emerged on the other side. The King's horsemen came as far as the river, but seeing that the couple had crossed the frontier, they returned. As soon as the maiden and the youth had crossed the water,

2 Navasard is the Armenian New Year, which falls on the 23rd of August.

and the Invulnerable Giant's castle appeared in the distance, the maiden said to the boy:

"Bedik, dearest, we have come so far and you have not yet spoken a single word to me; you have shown no sign of love. For Heaven's sake, tell me; did you kidnap me for yourself or for another?"

"You said, 'for Heaven's sake,'" replied the boy, "I will therefore tell you the truth; I have kidnaped you for the Invulnerable Giant; I have promised to deliver you to him."

"Alas!" exclaimed the maiden. "May Heaven's curse rest upon the Invulnerable! He could not get me for all the world. You do not reflect that it was by your skill and valor that you secured me. Woe be to frail womanhood! Maidens are the slaves of their hearts. For you, only for you, I eloped. If you reject me, here is the deep water, and here the high precipice; I would better be food for fishes and birds. May Heaven's fire burn and consume the hard hearts of men!" So saying, she prepared to throw herself down the abyss into the deep water. The boy's heart began to burn like a furnace, and he took hold of her, crying:

"No, dearest, do not harm yourself. It was because of the vow I made upon my soul that I am taking you to the Giant, and the day you become his wife I will put an end to my life with this sword, for without you life for me would be a curse."

Then they exchanged vows that they would use every means to put a speedy end to the Invulnerable Giant, and then be married; because they could not marry without destroying the Giant. Thereupon, they mounted the horse and began to proceed toward the castle. The Giant, who from the tower of the castle was looking their way, seeing them at a distance, immediately came down and ran to meet them. He expressed his gratitude to the boy, and his excess of love to the maiden. He treated her with extreme kindness, fearing that he might hurt her tender feelings with his unpolished manners.

"Are you pleased with this place?" he asked her. "What do you want me to do in order to make you as happy as possible?"

"I am very well, thank you; you are everything for me," said the maiden, suppressing her bitter hatred towards him. "But my parents consented to send me to you only under the condition that I should keep myself a virgin seven years longer. I have given an oath that I will do so; otherwise the love with which they have cherished me would turn into poison and defile my whole life. Do you accept this condition?"

"I do," said the Giant. "As you are now in my hand, I am willing to wait not only seven years, but, if necessary, seven times seven years."

They exchanged solemn vows, and decided that Bedik should live with them, and be the best man at their wedding. The maiden occupied one apartment of the castle, the youth and the Giant the other apartments, and so they lived for a time. But the boy and the maiden were uneasy. It was in vain to think of killing the Giant,--he was invulnerable. If they eloped he would certainly overtake them, and there was no escaping from his wrath. One day as the Giant was lying on the couch, with his head on the maiden's lap, she said to him:

"In former times, how did you live alone, without any companions? And how is it that you are invulnerable, when so many arrows and swords are thrown at you? What is the secret of your immortality?"

At first the Giant refused to tell, but the maiden importuned him, saying: "If you will not inform me, then you do not love me. Tell me in plain words that you love me not, and I will cease to live."

The Giant was at last persuaded to give up his secret, and he said:

"Seven days' journey from this castle there is a white mountain, where lives an unsubduable white bull which neither man nor beast dares to approach. Once in seven days he becomes thirsty and goes to the top of the white mountain, where there is a white fountain with seven white marble reservoirs full of water, which he drains at a single draught. The bull has in his belly a white fox, which in its turn has in its belly a white box made of mother-of-pearl. In that box are seven white sparrows. Those are my spirits, and those are my seven secrets. The bull cannot be subdued, the fox cannot be caught, the box cannot be opened, the sparrows cannot be seized. If either of them is taken, the others will escape. So I remain unconquerable and invulnerable and immortal."

The maiden told the secret to Bedik, adding:

"I have done what I could; now it remains for you to do the rest."

After a few days the boy girded on his sword, and bearing his bow and arrow, took leave of the Giant, saying that he would go on a month's journey. He started and went directly to the convent of the seven wise monks, who were renowned all over the world for their great erudition and learning. After performing his religious duties before the holy altar, he asked the monks:

"How is the unconquerable man conquered, and the unsubduable beast subdued?"

And he received the following answer

"Man by woman; beast by wine."

On the following day he loaded seven horses with seven skinfuls of seven-year-old wine and took them to the white mountain. He emptied the water out of the seven marble reservoirs and filled them with wine, turning the water of the fountain elsewhere. Near by he dug a trench, and hiding himself, waited for the result. At the end of seven days the white bull came to drink, and smelling the wine, he was so much terrified that he leaped as high as the height of seven poplar trees, and ran back roaring and bellowing. On the following day he returned, and being thirsty, drank the wine and was overcome. He leaped once or twice and fell down senseless. The boy drew his sword and approached and cut off the bull's head.

Let us return a moment to the palace of the Giant. It was the last day of the seven years during which he had waited for the maiden. He had gone to the hunt, that they might have noble game for their wedding dinner. When the bull was overcome and fell, the giant began to grow drowsy. As soon as the youth cut off the bull's head, the Giant turned dizzy, and a tremor ran through his frame.

"Alas!" cried the Giant. "Some one has killed the white bull. I know it is my fault. I gave my secret to the maiden, and she has told it to Bedik or to some other lover. The bull is killed, and I must die. I will go and kill the maiden. She is not to be for me; why shall she be for another?" So saying, he began to run toward the castle.

Bedik cut the bull's belly open; the fox also was drunk and stupid, and he cut off his head. The Giant lost his senses, and the blood began to gush out of his nostrils. The youth, opening the stomach of the fox, obtained the pearl box and put it in warm blood. The lid was opened, and the boy seized the seven sparrows. Thereupon streams of blood began to run from the Giant's mouth and ears, and his two eyeballs started from their sockets, like two great pomegranates. But still he was running toward the castle, sword in hand, and roaring like a mad beast. The maiden was horror-stricken, and quickly ran up to the top of the tower, determined to throw herself thence and kill herself, rather than fall into the hands of the Giant. The Giant had barely reached the castle door, when Bedik killed two of the sparrows; with that the two knees of the Giant were broken. He killed two more sparrows, and the Giant's two arms withered. He killed two more, and the lungs and heart of the Giant ceased to breathe and beat. He killed the last sparrow; the Giant knocked his head against the threshold of the castle, his skull was broken, and his brains oozed out. A black smoke rose from his mouth and nostrils, and he lay dead as a stone. Thereupon Bedik came on horseback like a flash of lightning. The maiden descended from the tower, and they embraced one another. At once they decided to go to the maiden's parents and celebrate their wedding. They collected all the wealth of the Invulnerable Giant, and mounting the horse of lightning, began to proceed toward the East.

The maiden being the only child of the King of the East, he was greatly grieved at her loss, seeing that he was getting old, and there was no successor to his throne. On the day following the maiden's disappearance, the King had sent his servants to the seven wise monks, asking their advice, and he had received the following message:

"The hero who carried off your daughter is a Prince. At the end of seven years your daughter will be restored to you by the same hero, as pure and chaste as before."

The anxious father waited for seven long years. It was

the last day of the seventh year; the King and his subjects had made great preparations for the reception of the returning Princess and her hero. Towards evening the King and his peers were looking anxiously from the seven towers of the city wall. The sun was just going down, when a flash as of lightning was seen on the western horizon, and in the twinkling of an eye Bedik and the maiden reached the city gate on the back of their fiery steed. They were received amid the wild acclamations of the crowd, and were led to the King's palace. There they knelt before the King and told their story. The King blessed them, and for forty days and forty nights the wedding feast was celebrated.

They attained their wish. May Heaven grant that you may attain your wishes!

Three apples fell from heaven—one for me, one for the story-teller, and one for him who entertained the company.

SIMON, THE FRIEND OF SNAKES

The King of the Snakes lives in the ruins of a big tower between Nineveh and Babylon, and rules all the snake tribe, both on land and sea. Once the King's son, who was viceroy of the province of Amida[1], wrote a letter to his royal father, as follows:

"Long live the King! May Heaven bestow upon you life everlasting. Amen. Be it known to you that your daughter-in-law and grandchildren were sick last summer, and the doctors advised that they must have a change of climate and must go to Mount Ararat and bathe in its pure streams, and eat its fragrant flowers, and this will immediately heal them. Consequently I sent her and the children, with their attendants, to Mount Ararat. I also wrote letters to the provincial viceroys and princes to assist the Princess and her train during their sojourn in that district. But the Prince of Aderbadagan[2], after receiving my letter, instead of giving help to the traveling Princess, collected his troops and assaulted her and her train. The attendants of the Princess met them bravely, and there, at the foot of Mount Ararat, occurred a bloody battle, which would doubtless have resulted in the total defeat of the Princess' train, on account of the superior numbers of the enemy, if a human being, Simon the Shepherd, who was tending his flock in a neighboring field, had not come to the assistance of our fatigued combatants. He took his great club, and entering

1 Amida corresponds to the modern province of Diyarbakir in Turkey.

2 The name of an ancient Armenian city and home of the Armenian monastery of St Thaddeus, currently an Armenian village in Iran named Qareh Kalisa.

the ranks of the warriors, beat and killed and pursued the assaulting brigands of the Prince of Aderbadagan, and saved the life of your daughter-in-law, who thus came safely through this perilous journey. You see, my liege, that there is good even among men. I will punish the vile Prince of Aderbadagan for his wicked conduct; but it remains for you to reward the goodness of this noble human being as you deem best, and oblige your affectionate son."

The King of the Snakes, receiving this letter, took with him a vast quantity of gold and jewels, and went to his palace, in a ruined castle between Aleppo and Amida. He posted his attendants on the highways to keep watch and inform him when Shepherd Simon should pass. The Shepherd was employed by dealers in livestock, who did business with Damascus and Aleppo, and was now on his way to Aleppo. As soon as he approached the palace of the Snake King the watchers informed their sovereign, and in the twinkling of an eye the whole army of snakes stood near the highway and began to conjure. Simon the Shepherd felt a strange dizziness—the heavens above and the earth below seemed to change. He stood there bewitched, while his companions drove away. Presently he opened his eyes, and lo! He was surrounded by innumerable snakes of all sizes and colors. Upon a golden throne was sitting a snake as thick as the body of an elephant, and upon his head there was a crown of costly jewels and diamonds. One of the snakes read a paper praising the goodness of the Shepherd, his natural fondness for the snake tribe, and his gallant defense of the weak and the wronged.

"Now, noble human being," said the King, "here is gold for you, precious jewels and diamonds; take as much as you like; and in addition to these, if you have a desire in your heart tell it to me and I will cause it to be satisfied."

Simon, after filling his shepherd's bag and his pockets with gold and jewels, said:

"I wish to understand the language of all animals, reptiles and birds."

"Let it be so," said the King; "but the day on which you shall tell anything of what you have seen or heard, you shall die."

The spell was removed, the snakes vanished, and Simon the Shepherd returned to his home near the foot of Mount Ararat. On the way he heard the animals talking, and lo! They knew all the secrets of men, and foretold events that would happen. Sometimes he laughed at what he heard, and sometimes he was terrified so that his hair stood erect upon his head. He entered his native village, and lo! All the dogs, cats, chickens, and even the long-legged storks were hallooing to one another and saying:

"Simon the Shepherd has come; his bag and pockets are full of gold and jewels."

Simon came to his house and put his treasure before his wife who, being a very curious woman, instantly asked him where and how he obtained so much wealth.

"Enjoy it, but never ask," answered Simon.

Simon heard his dog and chickens talking in regard to the secrets of his house. Some times he laughed and sometimes he was angry. His wife, noticing Simon's strange conduct towards the animals, asked the reason. He refused to tell, but she begged and importuned him, weeping all the time. Finally he could resist her entreaties no longer, and he promised to tell her everything on the following day. That evening he heard the dog talking to the cock, which was leading the chickens to roost, chuckling and gurgling:

"Tell me, master rooster," said the dog, "what is the use of your chuckling and gurgling, since our master has promised his wife to-morrow to tell her everything? He will die; people will come and kill you, shoot me, and plunder and ruin everything which belongs to our master."

"Eh! The sooner it is ruined the better," answered the rooster, contemptuously. "I have a family of forty wives, who are all obedient to me; if our master was as wise as he is rich, he would not pay attention to the vain inquisitiveness of his wife; he himself would not die, and no harm would befall us or his house. But now he deserves death."

Hearing this, Simon was advised; he seized his great club, and stood before his wife, saying:

"Wife, you must stop trying to compel me to tell you the secret; be content with what you have; else, by Heaven, I will beat you to death!"

The woman, seeing the club brandished over her head, put an end to her inquiries, and thereafter they enjoyed a happy life.

THE POOR WIDOW'S SON

Once upon a time there was a King who had a daughter who was quite beautiful. When she was of marriageable age the King sent heralds inviting all the young men of his realm to come to court in order that the Princess might make her selection. On the appointed day all the young men of the country passed before the Princess, who was standing with a golden apple in her hand that she might throw it at the choice of her heart. She threw the apple, and lo! It hit a poor widow's son. It was reported to the King, who was angry, and said:

"It cannot be; we must try it once more."

On the following day the Princess again threw the apple, and once more hit the same poor widow's son. On the third trial the same boy proved to be the maiden's choice. Thereupon the King was very angry, and expelled both the maiden and the boy from the court and the royal city. The boy took the maiden to the house of his mother, a poor old hut near the bridge without the city. The old widow, seeing the maiden, said to her son:

"We had not bread enough to keep us alive, and lo! You have brought a tender maiden. How shall we live now?"

"Be not angry, mamma," said the maiden, humbly, "I know how to spin yarn, and we shall be able to earn our living."

In this manner they lived a few months. Then they decided that the youth should travel and sojourn in other countries in order to earn money. On the following day they saw a merchant crossing the bridge with eighty camel-loads of merchandise destined for Arabia. The boy offered the merchant his services in the caravan. The merchant accepted, and the boy came home to make ready.

"Before you set out," said the bride, "go to yonder convent where there is a wise monk and ask him to give you some good advice, which you may need in your travels."

The boy went, and the old monk gave him the following maxims for his guidance:

First, "She whom one loves the best is the most beautiful;" secondly, "Patience leads to safety;" thirdly, "There is a good in every patient waiting."

He came back to his bride, who said:

"Commit these wise words to memory; you will no doubt have need of them."

"Farewell!" said the youth.

"Farewell!" said the young bride.

The boy departed from her. After a long journey the caravan camped in a desert near Arabia. There had camped before them also a large caravan composed of eighty other merchants. The boy was tired and soon fell into a deep sleep. There were many men and animals in the caravan, and all were thirsty. In that desert there was only one well, and that was dangerous; of all who had gone down to draw water, not one had ever come out. In the middle of the night, the boy was wakened by the crying of a herald in the caravan, who announced that each merchant was offering ten pieces of gold to the man who would descend into the well and draw water for men and animals. The boy, coveting the sum, promised to go down. His master pitied him, and tried to prevent him, but it was too late.

"You are going down into that dangerous well of your own free will," he said; "your blood shall be upon your own head. But if you come out safely, one of my camels shall be yours with the merchandise upon it."

They let the boy down with a rope. Reaching the bottom, he saw a flowing river of fresh water; he drank and quenched his thirst. Lifting up his eyes, nearby he saw a Giant sitting with a maiden on each side, one colored and the other white.

"Look, human being," exclaimed the Giant; "I will ask you a question. If you answer it rightly I will let you go; if not, I will kill you with this club, as I have killed so many men before you. Which of these two maidens is the beautiful one, and which the ugly?"

The boy remembered the first maxim of the old monk, and said: "She whom one loves the most is the most beautiful."

The Giant jumped up, and kissing the boy on the forehead, said: "Well done, youth! you gave me the only right answer; all the rest were wrong."

He then asked the boy the cause of his descent, and said:

"This well is enchanted; I must therefore give you a safe conduct. Take these three apples, and after drawing water enough, when you go up, drop one of these apples as soon as your feet are lifted from the ground; drop the second one when you reach the middle, and the third apple when you approach the well's mouth. Thus you will have a safe return."

And the Giant gave to the boy three pomegranates as a present, one white, one green and one red. The boy put them in his pockets, and after sending a sufficiency of water for the caravan, gave a sign to be drawn up. He threw the three apples just as he was directed by the Giant, and reached the surface safely. The merchants gave him the 800 pieces of gold and his master a camel's load of merchandise, as previously promised. The boy said to his master that he wanted to send the camel's load of merchandise and the money to his wife. His master consented, and the boy, putting the three pomegranates in the load, sent it with a driver to his hut near the bridge under the sycamore tree. The merchant promoted the boy, and made him superintendent of the camel drivers. After a time the merchant died, and his wife continued to do the business. She liked the boy and adopted him as her son. Thus he worked with that merchant and his wife for twenty years. One day he was granted permission by his adopted mother to go and visit his family, and he set out on his journey.

Leaving him on his way for a moment, let us turn to his family. A few months after the departure of the youth Heaven blessed his humble home by the birth of a son. When the camel's load of merchandise, money and pomegranates arrived, both the old widow and her young daughter-in-law were greatly pleased. At first sight the Princess knew that the pomegranates were not common fruits, but jewels; but the old widow, who thought they were common pomegranates, prepared to cut them, saying:

"Heaven's blessing rest upon you, my son, that you have remembered your aged mother by sending her fruits to eat!"

The bride snatched them from her hand and kept them in the drawer. Thereupon the old woman was offended, cursed her daughter-in-law and withdrew to the adjoining room. The bride ran to the neighboring shop, and buying three common pomegranates, brought them to her, saying:

"Mamma, be not offended; pardon my harsh conduct. Here are the pomegranates; you may eat them."

And mother and daughter were reconciled. The Princess then bought new dresses for her mother-in-law, herself, and the baby. She filled her mother-in-law's pocket with gold pieces, and cutting a slice from one of the pomegranates, put it in a costly golden box and gave it to her, saying:

"Now, mamma, go to the King's palace, and giving the gold pieces as a present to the attendants, say you want to see the King, and give him this golden box with the slice of pomegranate in it. When he asks you what you want, say that you have brought it to him as a present, and that you want nothing but a decree sealed with the royal seal, permitting you to do whatever you please without being molested."

The old woman, making herself as trim as she could, started on the errand and did all that the Princess had bid her. The King, upon seeing the jewels in the shape of a pomegranate slice, at once called the royal jewellers to set a price on them. The jewellers, examining the slice of pomegranate, said:

"No one can set a price on this. Let a boy of fifteen stand and throw a stone with all his might toward the sky; a heap of gold as high as that would hardly equal the value of this wonderful row of precious stones."

The King thought there was not so much gold in his treasury.

"Do you want the price of this jewel, or have you brought it as a present to the King?" asked the King of the woman.

"I have brought it as a present to your majesty," answered the woman.

"What favor do you want in recompense?" asked the King.

The old woman answered as she had been advised by her daughter-in-law. The royal decree was immediately signed, sealed, and given to the old woman, who brought it to her daughter-in-law. As soon as the Princess took the royal edict, she sent slices of the three pomegranates to all the seven Kings of the world and received in recompense treasure inestimable. She then built a splendid palace in the place of the poor old hut, and decorated it with silver, gold, and the rest of the jewels, which illumined the palace by night, making it as bright and lustrous as the twinkling morning star. The fame of this palace spread all over the world, and people came to see its splendor. The King also came to see it and admired it, because it contained so many beautiful things which were not to be found in his own palace. He visited all parts of it and sighed deeply from his heart, saying:

"I wish my only daughter was not lost, and that she lived in this magnificent building!"

From behind the curtain his daughter heard him speak, and she also sighed. The Princess' son had by this time grown into a good-looking, intelligent boy, and it was he who made a grand princely reception to the King in the new palace. The King greatly liked the boy and took him into his service. Seeing that he was an uncommon youth, displaying extraordinary ability in everything he handled, the King was so much pleased with him that he advanced him to the position of commander of his forces, without knowing that he was his own grandson.

Now let us return to the father of the commander. He arrived in his country and went directly in search of the bride, with the expectation of finding his lowly hut under the sycamore tree. But to his disappointment and surprise he found in its place a magnificent palace, the most magnificent indeed that he had seen in his travels of twenty years' duration. There was nothing left of the old hut, only the sycamore tree which had grown taller and thicker during the past twenty years. As a stranger he walked into the yard, approached the old sycamore tree, his only acquaintance in the neighborhood, and climbed it. Soon he saw a woman and the commander come to the porch and sit upon the sofa near one another. He knew the woman; she was his wife, the Princess. Twenty years seemed to have made little change in her. But why was she in this splendid palace and not in his hut? And what was the business of the commander there? Suspicion filled his mind, and he drew his bow and arrow with the intention of killing both of them. Just at that moment he remembered the old monk's second maxim—"Patience leads to safety," and he did not use his arms. Presently he saw the commander and his wife embracing one another. This time his blood ran to his brain and he drew his bow and arrow to shoot; but remembered the old monk's third maxim—"There is good in all patient waiting," and again he did not shoot. He began, however, to listen attentively to their talk, and heard the commander saying:

"Mother, is my father living? Where is he? Last night I dreamed in my dream that he had come home."

Thereupon his mother told him this entire story, which she had till then kept secret from him.

"What!" exclaimed the young commander, "you the daughter of the King; I the commander of his army; this palace our home, and my father a wanderer in foreign lands! It is impossible! I will to-morrow take my army and go and find my father."

His father, who was listening to his words from the tree, felt the great tears rolling down his cheeks. After nightfall he came down from the tree, and spent the night in a neighboring inn. The following morning he sent messages to his wife and son, bearing the good tidings of his arrival. Their meeting was a very happy one. The King, hearing of the return of his dear commander's father, hastened to express his congratulations and best wishes. Entering the palace he met, to his great surprise, his daughter, who with her husband and son fell on their knees, begging the blessing of the King. The old King was almost mad with joy, and embraced them all, shedding tears.

"Now I see," he exclaimed, "that it is useless to strive to undo what destiny has decreed. It was destined that you should marry one another, and lo! You prove to be the best match that I could desire."

As the King had no other child except that daughter, upon his death his son-in-law succeeded him upon the throne. Thus they reached the highest glory of this world. May Heaven grant that we may all reach the highest glory of the world to come!

A STINGY COMPANION

Two men were traveling in company on their way to a distant city. Each had a bag of food to support him on the journey, which would last several days. They agreed to first eat the provision of one man, and when that was finished to consume that of the other, which they expected would be sufficient to last during their journey. But when the store of the first man was finished, the second man would not allow his companion to use his own bag, as they had previously agreed.

"For Heaven's sake, Jack!" exclaimed the first man, "Give me something to eat. If you will not bestow it in return for my bread, give it as charity. Otherwise, I shall starve and die in this wilderness, while my family and children will be left paupers. Spare me, Jack, spare me!"

But it was impossible to persuade the second man, who refused, saying:

"No, I will give you nothing, lest the bread should not be enough for both. I will eat my own food and go. I don't care for you."

Can a hungry man walk? The one who had the provision bag went on ahead, leaving his starving companion behind. For a while the poor man walked, casting earth in his mouth and drinking water from every brook until sunset, when he came to a ruined mill.

"Let me lodge in this ruined mill," he thought. "Heaven is merciful."

There was nothing in the ruined mill, except an old tambourine that hung from the wall. In order not to be torn by wild beasts, the man entered the grain holder of the mill and tried to sleep. At midnight he saw a bear enter the mill and sit opposite the grain holder. Soon arrived a wolf, and took his seat near the bear, and at last came a fox, and sat next to the wolf. The wolf asked the bear, saying:

"How is it with you, brother bear? How do you fill that great stomach of yours, when game is so scarce nowadays?"

"I never am in trouble because of scarcity of food," answered the bear. "I find plenty of vegetables in the neighborhood, which have delicious roots. When I am hungry I dig some of these and appease my hunger."

"This is good!" thought the hungry man, in his concealment.

"And how is it with you, brother wolf," asked the fox. "Do you ever succeed in satisfying your gluttonous appetite, now that every shepherd keeps a cursed dog?"

"Oh, never mention that," answered the wolf, sighing deeply. "I have been planning all the time, during the past two or three months, to snatch some morsels from the flocks of the mayor of Greendale, but I never succeed in approaching the flock for fear of the big black dog, who never leaves the sheep. I do not know why the doctors do not kill that cursed dog, and bathe with its blood the King's son, who would at once be healed from the disease which has been tormenting him so long that the doctors have given up hope. By this means the poor boy would be cured and the obstacle before me would be removed."

"Good!" thought the man to himself.

"And how is it with you, brother fox?" asked the bear. "How are you getting along?"

"Gramercy!" said Reynard, "although I am not as strong as you are, yet Heaven has given me wisdom and dexterity, and I have never been troubled by hunger. Eh! I have accumulated some wealth also. I have a jug full of gold hidden under yonder sycamore tree, and another under the threshold of this mill. I get the gold pieces out once a day and enjoy myself in playing with them. Then I put them into the jugs and hide them once more."

"Very good!" said the man to himself.

The man took courage; his mind began to work; he suddenly took hold of the tambourine and began to play on it. Hearing this, the beasts ran away and disappeared in the twinkling of an eye. They thought a wedding procession was coming; and beasts are very much afraid of wedding processions. By this time it was daybreak. The man came out from his concealment, took the two jugs full of gold, filled his pockets, and hid the remainder in another place. He dug the roots which the bear had recommended and satisfied his hunger. He then asked the way to the village of Greendale and became a guest in the mayor's house. As he provided costly presents both for the mayor and the members of his family, they were all highly pleased with him. In the morning he heard the mayor whispering with the members of his family as to the present they could make their guest in recompense for his costly offerings. Thereupon the man said:

"I have admired the black dog of your flock; I wish I could have one like it."

"Since your desire is for that black dog," answered the mayor, "you may have it; we can easily find another dog for the flock."

The man put a rope around the neck of the dog, and taking with him a skin bottle, withdrew to a lonely place, where he cut the throat of the dog, and caught its blood in the skin. Taking the skinful of dog's blood, he went to the city and presenting himself to the King, said:

"I am a doctor; I can heal your son."

"If you can heal my son," said the King, "I will assure you the second place in the kingdom after my death; but if you do not heal him, I will cut off your head."

"May your son himself enjoy your throne," said the man; "but if I do not heal him my head is yours."

The King consented, and the man took the invalid Prince, who was very weak and upon his deathbed, to a room alone, where he applied the dog's blood over all his body, and laid him to sleep. Towards evening the boy had perspired and became wet all over. The assumed doctor washed him, and once more applied the dog's blood. He continued this treatment two days; on the third day the boy was cured, his body being as sound as that of a newly born babe. The man took the Prince to the King, who was so much pleased that he presented the physician with a magnificent palace, and abundant wealth. Not only the court but all the people of the country loved the man for his generous spirit. He sought and obtained the rest of the fox's treasure, which he had hidden, and caused his family to be brought to his new palace, where they lived a happy life, and praised Heaven.

But what became of his stingy companion, who had refused to give away a slice of bread? He reached his destination safely, but never attained success there, and was obliged to go from city to city seeking work to earn a living. At last he came to the city where his fortunate companion lived, and seeing him enjoying a princely life, asked him how he attained it. His former comrade told him everything. Thereupon the man hastened to the ruined mill, with the expectation that he also would attain good luck, and hid himself in the grain holder. The beasts again came to hold a meeting.

"Mr. Chairman," said Reynard to the bear, as soon as they came in, "before we commence our deliberations, we would better look carefully and see if there is a human being near by to hear us. Because I have been robbed since our last meeting."

They all got up to look around, and lo! There was a man in the grain holder.

"Vile intruder!" exclaimed the fox, biting the man's legs madly. The bear gave him some violent blows on the head with his heavy paws that made him fall senseless, and the wolf tore him into pieces. Thus ended the life of this stingy man.

THE MAIDEN OF THE SEA

There was an old woman and her son who lived on the seacoast. She used to cast a loaf of bread into the sea every morning. One day she said to her son:

"My son, I am getting old, and I feel that I shall soon die. Listen to my advice, and every morning cast a loaf of bread to the sea."

The old woman died, and the boy continued casting a loaf of bread into the sea every morning. One evening as he came back home from his work he was surprised to see the house swept and cleaned. Another day he put some meat in the cupboard, and in the evening, lo! the meat was cooked and the table ready for him. This was repeated several times. One day he hid himself under the stairs. Soon a splash of water was heard in the sea, and, lo! a big fish cast itself on the threshold. At once the skin of the fish fell down, and out of it came a maiden as beautiful as the shining moon. She swept the house clean, and finishing the kitchen work was just going out of the door, when the boy took hold of her.

"Mamma, mamma! Help me!" exclaimed the maiden. Immediately a voice came from the sea: "Be not afraid, daughter, that is my son-in-law." By the will of God and the permission of the mother, the maiden became the bride of the boy. At once the priest was called, who performed the marriage ceremony, and for seven days they celebrated the wedding festival.

One day, as the bride was working with a needle before the window, the Prince, who was taking a walk in his seashore orchard, saw her and was enchanted by her beauty. Finding out that she was a married woman, he decided to destroy her husband and get her in marriage. He immediately summoned the boy, and said:

"I want you to make me a tent so large that all my army may be accommodated in it, and yet half of it remain empty. I will give you three days' time to prepare it; if you don't make it ready by that time your head shall be cut off and all your property confiscated."

The boy came home with a sad face. What should he say to the Prince at the end of the third day? Surely his head should be cut off. The bride, seeing him, said:

"How now, husband! What is the matter? Why are you sad today?"

"Nothing," answered the boy, sighing.

"Nay, your face is changed," said the bride. "I pray you what is the matter?"

The boy told her what the Prince had ordered him to do.

"Never mind, husband," said she, and putting her head out of the window toward the sea, she cried:

"Mamma, mamma! Send us up our small tent, please. We want to go a-camping."

The small tent was thrown up from the sea. The boy took it to the Prince. It took his servants seven days to pitch it. Not only the Prince's army, but all his people were accommodated in it, and yet half of it was empty.

"This is right well," said the Prince, "but you see there is no furniture to put on the ground. I want you to bring me a rug to suit the tent exactly. If you don't bring it in three days your head shall be cut off."

The boy told his wife, and she asked her mother to send up the small rug, which was taken to the Prince. The Prince next day bade the boy fetch him a cluster of grapes so large that all his army might eat and not be able to finish it. On the following day that also was brought. Then the Prince wanted him to bring him a three-day old baby who could walk and talk like grown-up people. This time the boy was dismayed, because it was a sheer impossibility, and he thought he would surely lose his head this time.

"Never mind that, husband," said his wife, in the evening; and turning toward the sea, she cried:

"Mamma! Send up here the baby for a while, we want to see him."

The baby was given up, and the boy took him to the Prince, still doubting in his mind whether the baby could do what the Prince required. On the way the boy's foot slipped and the baby was shaken.

"Have you not your eyes about you, brother-in-law," the baby said, "or have you a mind to fall down and crush me under you?" The boy was pleased at the baby's reproach, because it assured him that his head would not be cut off. On being presented to the Prince the baby at once walked toward him, jumped up to his lap and giving the Prince a box on his ear, said:

"Are you not ashamed, Prince, to give so much trouble to my brother-in-law? You want to kill him and be married to my sister, do you? For shame, Prince, for shame!"

Thereupon the Prince gave up his evil intention, apologized to the boy and asked forgiveness. So the boy and his bride of the sea were left unmolested and they are still living on the border of the sea.

Three apples fell from heaven—one for me, one for the story-teller, and one for him who entertained the company.

HUSBAND OR WIFE?

A goldsmith and his wife lived a happy life in perfect harmony and love. In all the country they were considered the best patterns of conjugal love. It was their custom not to put out the light in their house but let it burn all the night. One night as the King and Queen were looking from their high window at the sleeping city, they noticed the goldsmith's light gleaming at a distance, and his well-known matrimonial love became the subject of debate between the royal couple. The King insisted that it was on account of the husband's virtue that he and his wife were in such perfect harmony. The Queen insisted that it was on account of the wife's virtue. Thereupon they decided to make a trial and find out the truth. On the following day the Queen sent one of her handmaids to the goldsmith, saying that she had fallen in love with him and would become his wife if he killed his present wife.

"Not I," answered the goldsmith; "I will not part from my wife for all the world. I am content with what Heaven has assigned me. I will not exchange my wife for a thousand Queens."

On the following day the King sent a servant to the goldsmith's wife, saying that he had been charmed with her beauty and wanted to make her queen, if she would kill her present husband.

"Is it really true? Is it really true?" exclaimed the woman.

"It is true," answered the servant.

"Well, then," said the woman, "I will kill my husband this very night. When you see our light has gone out tonight, know that I have begun to murder him."

The servant brought word to the King, who ordered his

men to be ready and go to the rescue of the goldsmith if the light was really put out. In the evening the goldsmith came home. After supper the husband and wife had a nice talk as usual, and the husband, putting his head in the lap of his wife, fell asleep. The woman put the loop of a rope around his neck, blew out the candle, and began to pull the rope. The poor goldsmith was strangled before the King's men came to the rescue. This murder of one of his best subjects grieved the King so deeply that he thereafter hated all women from the depths of his soul. He could not sleep that night, and early in the morning he called his prime minister, saying:

"Today I will go hunting. You must put to death all the women of the country, old and young, before I come home this evening."

The prime minister had an aged father, to whom he went and repeated the King's terrible order.

"Do not obey it," said the old man; "I shall be responsible. Go and hide yourself for a couple of days from the anger of the King."

In the evening the King came back from hunting, and seeing the women of the realm still alive, was enraged, and called his prime minister into his presence. The old man appeared before the King, standing on his crutches.

"Where is your son?" said the King. "I want to cut off his head first, then those of the women."

"Long live the King!" said the old man with his trembling voice. "Permit me to tell you an experience of mine, and then put your command into execution if you choose."

"Speak!" said the King, who at the same time gave orders to the soldiers to be ready to butcher the women.

"I was prime minister during your father's reign," said

the old man. "One day we had gone to hunt. I was led astray by the game, and came near a village on the other side of the forest. Soon I was overtaken by an unknown horseman, who took hold of me, and lifting me from the back of my horse, placed me before him upon the saddle of his own horse, bound me with a rope, and tied the reins of my horse to the back of his own. To struggle on my part was useless, because he was very strong. Soon we arrived at a cemetery, where we dismounted. For a while he looked here and there, and stopping at a certain place, began to dig, and ordered me to shovel the earth after him. Thus working we dug two graves. We mounted again and dismounted at the foot of a castle wall. He bound me carefully to the saddle of his horse, and himself climbed up the wall. After a few minutes he threw down from the top of the wall the headless corpse of a man who had just been murdered. He came down, and placing the corpse on my horse took it and myself to the graves we had dug. I was horror stricken, and thought that one of the graves must be for the corpse and the other for me. But to my surprise, he untied me and bade me assist him to bury the corpse, which I did. He then turned to me and said:

"'I know who you are; you are the prime minister of this state. Now listen to me, and go and tell the King my story. I am a woman and had a boundless love for my husband. This vile Prince, whose body we have just now buried, having fallen in love with me, killed my own husband that he might win my love. But I vowed by the sacred love I bore my husband to kill the murderer and bury him under my husband's feet. Now that is accomplished. I vowed next to kill myself, that I might be buried by the side of my husband. For the love of Heaven, bury me in this grave and tell my story to the King.' This she said, and stabbing herself with a dagger, fell dead at my feet. I buried her in that grave near her husband. Here you have the example of a faithful and brave wife. If the unfaithful wife of the goldsmith gave you occasion to order the death of all the women of the realm, let this woman be the means of saving her sex from general slaughter. Why shall many good women die because of the wickedness of one woman?"

Thereupon the King revoked the order and only the goldsmith's wife was put to death.

THE WICKED STEPMOTHER

Once upon a time, in Armenia, there was a noted hunter, who was a widower. He had a son by a former wife. He married another wife, but soon was taken mortally sick. On his deathbed he said to his wife:

"Wife, I am dying, and I know that when my son grows up he will follow my profession. Take care and do not let him go to the Black Mountains to hunt."

After the death of the hunter, the son growing up, began to follow his father's profession, and became a hunter. One day his stepmother said:

"Son, your father, when dying, said that after you grew up, if you followed his profession, you should not go to the Black Mountains to hunt."

But the boy, paying no attention to what his father had advised him, one day took his bow and arrow, mounted his horse and hastened to the Black Mountains to hunt. As soon as he reached them, lo, a giant made his appearance on the back of his horse of lightning, and exclaimed:

"How now! Have you never heard my name, that you have dared to come and hunt on my ground?" And he threw three terrible maces at the boy, who very cleverly avoided them, hiding himself under the belly of his horse.

Now it was his turn; he drew his bow and arrow, took aim and shot the giant, who was nailed to the ground. He at once mounted the giant's horse of lightning, which galloping, soon brought him to a magnificent palace, gilded all over with gold and decorated with precious jewels. Lo, a maiden as beautiful as the sun appeared in the window, saying:

"Human being, the snake upon its belly and the bird

with its wing could not come here; how could you venture to come?"

"Your love brought me hither, fair creature," answered the boy, who had already fallen in love with the charming maiden.

"But the giant will come and tear you into pieces," said the maiden, who also had fallen in love with the boy.

"I have killed him, and there lies his carcass," answered the boy.

The door of the palace was opened, and the boy was received by the maiden, who told him that she was the daughter of a Prince, and that the giant had stolen her and kept her in that palace, where she had forty beautiful handmaids serving her.

"And as you have killed the giant," she added, "I, who am a virgin, shall be your wife, and all these maidens will serve us." And they accepted one another as husband and wife.

Opening the treasures of the giant, they found innumerable jewels, gold, silver, and all kinds of wealth. The boy thought such a beautiful palace, with so many treasures worthy of a prince, and the most beautiful wife in the world, things that he could hardly have dreamed of, and he decided to live there, going to hunt every day as usual.

One day, however, he came home sighing, "Ah! Alas! Alas!"

"How now, what is the matter?" said the beautiful bride. "Am I and my forty handmaids not enough to please you? Why did you sigh?"

"You are sweet, my love," said the boy, "but my mother also is sweet. You have your place in my heart, but my mother also has her place. I remembered her, therefore I sighed."

"Well," said the young bride, "take a horseload of gold to your mother, let her live in abundance and be happy."

"No," said the boy, "let me go and bring her here."

"Very well, go, then," said the young bride.

The boy went to his stepmother and telling her all that he had done, brought her to the palace of the Black Mountains. There she was the mother-in-law of the fair bride, and therefore the superior of the whole palace. Both the bride and the maidens had to submit to her.

The boy used to go out hunting. The stepmother, being well versed in witchcraft and medicine, went secretly, and administered some remedy to the corpse of the giant, so that he was soon healed. Falling in love with the giant, she took him to the palace and hid him in the cellar, where she secretly paid him daily visits, as she was afraid of her stepson. Wishing, however, to have none to oppose her, the witch one day said to the giant:

"Giant, you must advise me of a way by which I may send my son on an errand, and from which he may never come back."

Upon the advice of the giant, she entered her room and putting under her bed pieces of very thin and dry Oriental bread, lay down upon the bed and feigned sickness. In the evening the boy returned from hunting, and hearing that his stepmother was ill, hastened to her side, and asked:

"What is the matter, mother?"

"O, son," exclaimed the witch, with a sickly voice, "I am very sick. I shall die," and as she turned from one side to the other the dry bread began to crackle.

"Hark!" exclaimed the witch, "how my bones are crackling!"

"What is the remedy, mother, what can I do for you?" asked the boy.

"O, my son," said the witch, "there is only one remedy for my sickness, and that is the Melon of Life. I shall never be healed, if I do not eat one of that fruit which you could bring to me."

"All right, mother," said the boy, "I will bring to you the Melon of Life."

He at once started upon the expedition, and after a long journey was guest in the house of an old woman who asked him where he was going. When she heard of the errand, she said to the boy:

"Son, you are deceived; the expedition is a fatal one—do not go."

But as the boy insisted, the old woman said:

"Well, then, let me advise you. On your way you will soon come to a mansion, which is the abode of forty giants, who in the daytime go out hunting. But you will find their lady there kneading dough. If you are agile enough to run and suck the nipples of the open breast of that giantess without being seen by her, you are safe; if not, she will make one mouthful of you and devour you."

The boy went and found as foretold by the old woman. He was clever enough to suck the nipples of the giantess without being seen by her.

"A plague on her who advised you!" exclaimed the angry giantess, "else I would make a good morsel of you. But now having sucked of my breast, you are like one of my own sons. Let me hide you in a box, lest the forty giants should come in the evening and finding you here, devour you."

And she shut the boy in a box. In the evening the forty

giants came, and smelling a human being, said:

"O mother, all the year long we hunt beasts and fowls which we bring home to eat together, and now we smell a human being, whom no doubt you have devoured to-day. Have you not preserved for us at least a few bones which we might chew?"

"It is you," answered the lady, "that are coming from mountains and plains where no doubt you have found human beings, and the smell comes out of your own mouths. I have eaten no human being."

"Yes, mother, you have," exclaimed the giants.

"How if my nephew, the son of my human sister, has come to pay me a visit!" answered the giantess.

"O mother," exclaimed the giants, "show us our human cousin; we will not hurt him, but talk with him."

The giantess took the boy out of the box and brought him to the giants, who were very much pleased to see a human being so small, but so beautiful and manly. Holding him up like a toy, the giants handed him to one another to gratify their curiosity by looking at him.

"Mother, what has our cousin come for?" inquired the giants.

"He has come," answered the giantess, "to pick a Melon of Life, and carry it to his mother who is sick. You must go and get the Melon of Life for him."

"Not we," exclaimed the forty giants, "it is above our ability."

The youngest of the forty brothers, however, who was lame, said to the boy:

"Cousin, I will go with you and get the Melon of Life for you. You must only take with you a jug, a comb, and a razor."

On the following day the boy took what was necessary and followed the lame giant, who soon brought him to the garden of the Melon of Life, which was guarded by fifty giants. The guards being asleep, the boy and his companion entered the garden without being perceived, and picking the Melon began to run. But they were just crossing the hedges, when the lame leg of the giant was caught by the fence, and in his haste to release it he shook the hedges which crackled like thunder and, lo, all the fifty giants awoke crying:

"Thieves! human beings! a good prey for us!" and began to pursue the boy and his lame companion.

"Throw the jug behind you, cousin," exclaimed the lame giant.

The boy did so, and lo, plains and mountains behind them were covered by an immense sea that the fifty giants had to cross in order to reach them. By this means they gained quite a distance till the fifty crossed the sea.

"Now, cousin, throw the comb behind you," exclaimed the lame giant.

The boy did so, and lo, an extensive jungle between them and the fifty giants. They gained another great distance before the giants finished crossing the jungle.

"Throw the razor now, cousin," exclaimed the lame giant.

The boy did so, and lo, all the country between them and the fifty giants was covered with pieces of glass, sharp as razors. Before the fifty could cross the distance the thirty-nine giants came to the rescue of the two and took them, safely to their borders.

The boy took leave of his adopted aunt and cousins, find taking the Melon of Life with him, returned home. On his way, however, he was again the guest of the old woman, who seeing him come safely, asked if he had succeeded in bringing the precious fruit.

"Yes, I have brought it, auntie," answered the boy, and told her his tale.

In the middle of the night, when the boy was sound asleep, the old woman took the Melon of Life out of the boy's saddlebag and put a common melon in its place. In the morning the boy brought the melon to his stepmother, who eating it exclaimed:

"O, happy! I am healed."

The boy again went hunting, and the witch said to the giant:

"Look here, giant; this enterprise did not prove fatal to my stepson. Advise me of another more dangerous journey on which I may send him, and from which he shall surely not return."

Upon the advice of the giant she once more placed some thin and dry loaves of bread under her bed and lay down feigning sickness. In the evening when the boy came she said in a weak voice:

"O, son, I am dying, you will not see me any more."

"Why, mother," exclaimed the boy, "what is the matter? What can I do for you?"

"The only remedy for my sickness," answered the witch, "is the milk of the Fairy Lioness. If you bring it for me I shall live; if not, I must die."

The boy started, and again was the guest of the old woman, who asked where he was going.

"I am going this time to bring a skinful of the milk of the Fairy Lioness for my mother," answered the boy.

The old lady again importuned him not to go, but as he insisted she said:

"Well, as you are resolved to go, let me advise you. On the other side of yonder mountain is the den of the Fairy Lioness, which is at this moment very much troubled by a pustule on her paw, and you will find her at the entrance of her den, holding her pustulous paw above her head and roaring. Now, you must approach her cleverly without being noticed by her, and taking aim with your bow and arrow, shoot into the pustule, which, being wounded, will at first cause her great pain and make her roar. But soon the pain being past, she will feel comfortable and give you whatever you demand of her."

The boy went, and found the Fairy Lioness, as foretold by the old lady, standing at the entrance of her cave, and roaring on account of her pain. The boy at once taking aim, shot and wounded the pustule. The pain of the Lioness increasing she exclaimed:

"Oh! who was it that shot this arrow? I would I could find him and devour him. Oh! Oh! Oh!"

But soon, the matter of the wound coming out, she felt comfortable, and said:

"Who was it that shot this arrow? By Heaven, I would give him whatever he demanded."

The boy at once jumping out from his concealment stood before the Lioness, who seeing him exclaimed:

"Was it you, young hero, that healed me of my pain which was troubling me so long?"

"Yes, it was I," answered the boy.

"Demand of me whatever you please," said the Lioness, "I am ready to give to such a hero as you anything that you may ask."

"Give me," said the boy, "some milk of your own udders, which is the only remedy to heal my sick mother."

"In yonder cave," said the Lioness, "there are two orphan cubs; go kill them, and flaying them, bring the skins to me."

The boy did so and brought her the two whole skins. The Lioness milked her udders into them until they were filled.

"Here," said the Lioness, "take these and go, and be careful not to harm my little cubs on your way."

The boy took the two cubs' skins full of milk and thanking the Lioness, departed. On his way, however, he slily stole two beautiful cubs and began to run. But the mother Lioness smelling her young ones, pursued the boy, and overtaking him, exclaimed:

"How now, human being! is this the way you reward kindness done to you? Why did you steal my two cubs?"

"I humbly beg your pardon," answered the boy. "I was so much pleased with your kindness that I wanted to have a permanent keepsake from you, and what better thing could I carry with me than a brace of your cubs, which I will nourish on princely diet and keep as faithful friends."

The Lioness, being much pleased with this answer, gave him leave to carry the cubs. He soon came to his hostess, who asked if he brought the Fairy Lioness's milk.

"Yes, auntie, I have brought it," answered the boy, presenting the two skins full of milk.

During the night, however, when the boy was sound asleep, the old woman poured out the Lioness's milk from the skins into a cask and filled them with common goat's milk. On the following day, the boy, loading the skins on the back of his horse, took the cubs and went home. The stepmother, drinking the milk, exclaimed:

"O good! I am healed."

The boy again went hunting as usual. The witch said to the giant:

"Giant, did I not tell you to advise me and name a task from which my stepson would never return? Why are you devising only light tasks, which he can so easily accomplish? Now you must either advise me as to the most dangerous expedition in which he will surely lose his life, or I will betray you to him and he will cut you into pieces."

"What can I do?" replied the giant, "your son is the bravest hero that ever lived; no mortal can vanquish him. He will return from any expedition, no matter how dangerous it may be. Let him go this time and bring you a jug full of the Water of Life."

The witch again feigned sickness, and when the boy came to see her she said:

"O my son, I am dying, my bones are breaking," and the crackling of the dry bread under the bed was heard when she turned from one side to the other.

"What shall I do for you, mother?" asked the boy sadly.

"The only remedy for me this time," answered the witch, "is the Water of Life, and you must go and bring to me a jug full, else I shall die."

The boy at once mounted his horse and taking with him the two cubs, which by that time had grown up to be a pair of fine young lions, he went to his hostess and explained the object of his expedition.

"O son," exclaimed the good woman, "I see plainly that you are employed for some wicked purpose; there must be a detestable plot against your life. This is the most dangerous expedition that ever human being has undertaken, and no one has ever returned from the task you have started upon. Be advised, go back; your mother is surely false."

"Not I," said the boy, "I will certainly go."

The old woman said, "As soon as you place your jug in the fountain to receive the water, which oozes out only in the thickness of a hair, a heavy sleep will fall upon you, and you will remain there benumbed for seven days and nights. First, scorpions will assail you; then serpents; then beasts of prey, and at last all kinds of genii. You will surely be devoured by them."

"Let come what may, I will go," said the boy, and taking the two lions with him, he started for the fountain of the Water of Life.

He came to the fountain and found the water oozing out in a tiny stream. As soon as he placed his jug under it, a sound sleep overpowered his senses and he remained there benumbed for seven days and seven nights. Soon innumerable large scorpions began to attack the sleeping hero. But the lions destroyed all of them. Then thousands of terrible serpents made their appearance and assailed the boy, hissing and striking with their forked tongues. The lions, after a bloody fight, destroyed them also. Soon a whole army of voracious beasts surrounded the fountain in search of the boy. The lions, after a sanguinary strife, succeeded in destroying them also.

At the end of the seven days and nights, the boy awoke, and to his great horror saw that he was surrounded by a high wall that the lions had built of the carcasses of the beasts and serpents they had killed. The two faithful guardians were now sitting on either side of their master and were watching his every motion. The boy, seeing them stained with blood from head to foot, understood how much he owed to them in the preservation of his life. He then washed them clean with the Water of Life and taking the jug, which by that time was filled, he returned to his hostess.

"Did you bring the Water of Life?" asked the old lady.

"Yes, auntie, I did," answered the boy, presenting her the jug full of water.

"It was not you that succeeded," returned the old woman, "but Heaven and your faithful lions that preserved your life."

During the night, as the boy was sleeping, the old woman poured the Water of Life into another vase, and filled the jug with common water, which the boy in the morning took to his stepmother, who drinking it said:

"O, happy! I am healed."

The following day the boy again went hunting. The witch said to the giant:

"Can you not devise some means to destroy my stepson? By Heaven, I will destroy you this time if you do not tell me how to destroy him."

"Your stepson is brave," answered the giant, "he is a unique hero, and no one can kill him but yourself."

"How! how!" exclaimed the witch with great joy, "tell me and I will do it."

"Do you not remember the three red hairs among his black hairs on his head? As soon as they are picked, your son dies."

On the following day the witch said to the boy:

"Come, son, lay your head in my lap and take a nap."

The boy did so and soon slept. The witch immediately took hold of the three red hairs and picked them out. A spasm or two, and the hero died.

"Now, giant," said the witch, "take that sword and chop this corpse into small pieces."

"Not I," answered the giant, "my hand will not be lifted to chop such a hero."

"You coward!" exclaimed the witch, and taking the sword she chopped the corpse into small pieces, put these into a sack, and threw them over the garden wall. One of the little fingers, however, fell into the garden.

The lions learned that their master was killed, and that his chopped body had been put into the bag. They immediately took hold of the bag and carried it to the old woman, the hostess of the hero. Opening the bag, she took out the body, and putting every part in its proper place made a whole; only the little finger was missing. She explained to the lions what was missing, and they at once went, and smelling their master's finger in the garden, found it and brought it to the old woman, who put it in its proper place. Now she brought the milk of the

Fairy Lioness, which she had secretly preserved, and poured it over the body. Immediately all the broken bones, muscles and sinews came together, and all the members being united, the body became as sound and delicate as that of a newborn babe. Then she brought the Melon of Life, and put it before his nostrils. As soon as the boy smelt it, he sneezed seven times. Then she poured the Water of Life down his throat. At once the boy opened his eyes, and jumped up, saying:

"O, what a sound sleep was this that overpowered my senses!"

"Sleep!" exclaimed the kind woman. "Yes, a sleep out of which you would never have awaked had not Providence preserved you." And she told him what had happened.

"Now, my good hostess," said the boy, "you have done me a very great kindness—a kindness that I can never reward. May Heaven reward you!"

He brought her from his treasures a horseload of gold and a horseload of silver, saying:

"These are for you; spend as much as you like and pray for me as long as you live."

The boy came to his palace and found that his beautiful bride was imprisoned in a dark cellar, where she was left to starve, while the witch, his stepmother, was in an excess of merriment with the giant and half a dozen younglings around her. They were all amazed to see the hero enter, and the giant was about to make his exit through a secret door in the wall when the boy seized hold of him, saying:

"How now, coward, are you running? Stop and solve this puzzle for me; whose are these ugly younglings that are infecting the very air of my palace?"

"They are my children out of yonder woman, your mother," answered the giant.

"Mother! I have no mother," exclaimed the boy. "You increase so soon, do you? Now we are going to have great merriment. Go and bring me from yonder mountain, wood enough to build a large pile."

The giant obeyed, and soon a large pile of wood was built in the courtyard of the palace. The boy struck a flint and lighted the wood. Soon the whole pile was on fire, burning like a furnace.

"Now, giant," said the boy, "take hold of these bastards, and throw them into the fire, one by one."

The giant obeyed, and all the younglings were burned on the pile.

"Bring now yonder witch, and throw her into the fire," ordered the boy. She also shared the fate of the bastard children.

"Now, shall I throw you also?" asked the boy of the giant.

"Hero," exclaimed the giant, "I honor you, I will obey you."

"Well, then," said the boy, "I will not kill you. Come, pass under my sword and swear obedience to me."

The giant kissed the sword, and passing under it became the bondman of the boy.

The boy then released his beautiful wife from the dark prison. They celebrated anew their nuptials for forty days and forty nights, and enjoyed a happy life thereafter.

Thus they attained their wishes. May Heaven grant that you may attain your wishes!

Three apples fell from heaven—one for me, one for the story-teller, and one for him who entertained the company.

THE TRICKS OF A WOMAN

Sarkis was a simple farmer who prayed every morning before he went to the fields, and every evening after he came from his work. One day his wife said to him:

"Husband, why do you not mention in your prayer that God may preserve you from the tricks of a woman?"

"Tricks of a woman?" exclaimed the man. "I am not such a coward as to be afraid of a woman or her tricks."

"Is that your opinion of a woman?" asked his wife.

"Yes, that is my opinion of a woman," answered Sarkis sternly, as he shouldered his farming utensils.

The woman decided to give her husband proof of a woman's power, so she bought some fish, and putting them in her apron, took them to the farm at noon, when she carried her husband's dinner. The farmer went to the bank of a neighboring brook to eat his dinner, when his wife, taking advantage of his absence, buried the fish here and there in the field, and went home. Soon Sarkis returned to his ploughing, and as the earth was turned, lo! Fish came out of the ground. He picked them up, and in the evening, bringing them home to his wife, told her that he had taken them from the farm and that he believed the Creator had created them in that very place. He then ordered his wife to cook them, and on the following day bring them to the farm for his dinner. On the morrow, the woman cooked the fish, ate them herself, and took to her husband a bowl of pea soup for his dinner.

"Where are the fish?" asked Sarkis.

"Fish! What fish?" exclaimed the woman, feigning surprise.

"Why, the fish which I picked from the farm yesterday,"

said the farmer.

"Are you crazy, husband?" said she, "you have not brought home any fish that I know of."

"What!" exclaimed Sarkis, taking hold of the whip, "you have eaten my fish, and do you call me crazy?" and he threatened to beat her.

"Help!" exclaimed the woman, and ran to a neighbor's farm.

Thereupon the ploughmen of the neighborhood came to the rescue of the woman and took hold of Sarkis.

"Nay, let me beat her to death," said Sarkis; "she has eaten my fish, and now she calls me crazy."

The ploughmen asked the woman what fish he meant.

"Nay, I beseech you," exclaimed the woman, "take hold of him, don't let him go; he will kill me. Woe upon me! He is certainly crazy, he is a lunatic. Ask him where he found the fish he talks of."

"Why, I caught them just here," said Sarkis. "I dug them from the ground."

"Alas!" exclaimed the ploughmen; "the woman is right, he has really lost his mind."

And as they bound him with ropes some of the farmers said:

"He of late has been giving signs of this."

"It is a hereditary disease," said some others, "many members of his family have been crazy."

So, treating the poor man as a lunatic, they brought him to his home and bound him to a pillar after whipping him. At night, when everybody else had gone, the woman approached her husband, saying:

"How now, husband? Are you afraid of a woman's tricks or not? This was the least of all."

"For Heaven's sake, wife, untie me," said Sarkis in a pitiful voice. "Be sure my first prayer hereafter shall be to be preserved from a woman's tricks."

She released him and thereafter he was wise as respects women.

A WISE WEAVER

A king was once sitting upon his throne when an ambassador from a distant country approached, drew a line around the throne, and sat down without speaking a word. The King did not understand this mystery. He called his ministers. They also did not understand it. It was a disgrace to the King that he did not have a man wise enough to understand the symbolical message of a neighboring sovereign. The King was very angry, and ordered his ministers to solve the riddle themselves, or to find some one in the city to solve it immediately; otherwise he would put them all to death. Thereupon the ministers began to search through the realm for a wise man. After a long quest they came to a certain house, which they entered. There was no one in the first room but a baby sleeping in a cradle. And strange to say, the cradle was rocking without any visible cause. They entered the adjacent room, and lo! there also was a baby sleeping in a cradle, which was rocking, though no one was in the room. They walked out into the back yard, where they saw wheat washed and spread to dry; there was a cane moving to and fro, driving away the sparrows, in order that they might not eat the wheat. The ministers of the King were surprised, and going down into the cellar they found a weaver weaving cloth. As his wife had died soon, after giving birth to twins, he had both to weave for his living and do a housewife's work and nurse his children. He therefore had connected the two cradles and the sparrow driver to his loom and shuttle with cords; and so, in this manner, by virtue of his cleverness he was performing all his duties without much trouble. The ministers thought that this man might solve the King's riddle, and so they told him what had happened. The weaver thought a while and then taking a couple of marbles and a chicken, went with the ministers. Entering the presence of the King, he looked the foreign ambassador in the face, and threw before him the marbles. The ambassador took from his pocket a handful of grain and spread it on the floor. The weaver put down the chicken, which in a few minutes ate all the grain. Thereupon the ambassador put on his sandals and ran away speedily.

"What was all this?" asked the King.

"By drawing the line around the throne," answered the weaver, "the ambassador wished to say that their King was coming to besiege us, if we did not humiliate ourselves and pay tribute. To this I answered by dropping marbles, which meant that they were children compared to ourselves and that they would better go and play marbles, rather than to undertake a war which would result in their utter ruin. By spreading the handful of grain he meant that their forces were innumerable. By the chicken which ate all the grain, I meant that a company of ours was enough to destroy a legion of theirs."

The King was pleased with the weaver, and gave him costly presents, but the weaver took only a little to enable him to bring up his beloved twins. The King wanted to make him his prime minister, but the weaver declined, saying:

"Let me continue to be a weaver; only I beg you to remember, that wisdom and understanding are not distributed according to rank and that the common tradesmen are entitled to be treated as humanely as your peers and noblemen."

MIND OR LUCK?

Mind and Luck were one day debating.

"It is only by me that a man becomes a man," said Luck.

"No, it is by me," insisted Mind. At last they decided to make a trial upon a villager who was working on a neighboring farm. Luck first approached the man, and lo! the ploughshare unearthed a jug. The farmer stopped, and opening the mouth of the jug saw that it was full of gold coins.

"Ah!" he exclaimed, "I shall be a rich man." But soon he changed his mind and said,--"Yes, but how will it be if thieves hear about my wealth, and come and rob me, and upon my resistance, kill me?"

While he was thus musing, he saw the judge passing by, on his way to the village. He at once decided to give the gold to the judge, and himself continue to live his tranquil farmer's life. Accordingly he ran and called the judge to the farm. But before the judge had arrived, Mind had entered the man's brain. He hid the jug and said to the judge:

"Sir, you are a judge, you are a learned man; do tell me, which of these two oxen of mine is the better one?"

The judge was angry and departed scolding the man. Mind also departed, and the farmer began to soliloquize:

"Oh, what a blockhead I am! why did I not give the gold to the judge? Surely he was the best man to have it. What shall I do with these coins? Where shall I keep them?"

He did not work during the rest of the day, but spent his time in useless meditation. In the evening he saw the judge returning from the village. He ran to meet him and begged him to come to his farm for a moment. The judge thought there must be meaning in the man's conduct, and entered the field.

By that time Mind had returned to the man's brain, and he said to the judge:

"Sir, you are a learned man; do tell me which is the larger, the lot which I ploughed yesterday or the one I ploughed to-day?"

The judge thought that the man was crazy and departed smiling. Mind also departed from the man, who began to beat his head, saying:

"What a pumpkin-pated fellow I am! Why did I not give the gold to him? Where shall I keep it? What shall I do with it?"

So saying he placed the jug in his lunch-bag, and came home leading the oxen.

"Wife! O wife!" he exclaimed; "lead the oxen to the stable, give them hay, and take the plough in. I will go to the judge and come back."

His wife, a shrewd woman, saw that there was something in the lunch-bag which her husband did not put down. It must be something which she thought she ought to know, so she said to him:

"It is not my business to take care of your oxen. I have hardly time enough to drive and milk the cows, and care for the sheep. You put in your oxen and plough, and go wherever you please."

The man, putting the lunch-bag by the door, began to attend to his oxen. While he was thus occupied, the woman opened the bag, and seeing the jug full of gold, took it out and put a round stone in its place. The man then took the bag to the judge, and placing it before him, said:

"I have brought you this as a present." On opening it they saw that it was a stone. The judge was angry with the man, but thinking that he might after all have a secret, he cast him into prison. He put two spies in his cell to watch the man and report whatever he did or said. The man began to meditate in the jail, motioning with his hands:

"The jug was as big as this, its mouth as wide as this, its belly as large as this, and the gold in it as much as this."

The spies reported to the judge that the man was making certain gestures, but not speaking. The judge called the man and asked what it was he was showing with his hands. Mind entered the man's brain, and he answered:

"I was thinking to myself that you had a head as big as this, a neck as thick as this, a beard as long as this. And I was asking myself whose pate and beard was the larger, yours or our goat's?"

Thereupon the judge was very angry and ordered his men to beat the farmer to death. The thrashing was hardly begun when the man exclaimed:

"Do not beat me, I will tell the truth."

They ceased beating him, and brought him to the judge, who asked him to tell the truth as to what he was measuring in the jail.

"The truth is this," said the man, "that if you continued to beat me I would surely die."

This made the judge laugh, and he ordered the man to be released, being convinced that he was only a lunatic. The man came safely home. Thereupon Mind and Luck shook hands and made friends, saying:

"Luck with Mind, Mind with Luck, can make a man a man."

THE WORLD'S BEAUTY

A rich merchant of the city of Baghdad had accumulated great wealth and property. He had a wife and a son. One day the merchant fell sick, and felt that he was about to die. On his deathbed he called his son, saying:

"You see, my son, I have accumulated so great wealth that even princes have not as much. I bequeath all to you. Continue my business and enjoy your property, but never go to the city of Tiflis[1]."

Then he called his wife, explained to her the mystery of his riches, and gave her the key of his secret chamber, saying:

"If my son spends all my wealth and becomes poor, then you may tell him my secrets."

The merchant died, and his son, continuing his business, one day took forty camel-loads of merchandise, and set out for the city of Erzerum. In the caravansary, where he deposited his goods in Erzerum, he met two poor men in rags, sighing and beating their breasts.

"What is the matter with you?" asked the young merchant.

"Oh!" exclaimed the two ragamuffins, "It is something that cannot be told."

The boy had great compassion on them, and said:

"Nay, masters, tell me your grief; I am ready to spend all my wealth for your sake."

At last they said:

"Would to heaven you had not met us, sir! You will be like ourselves."

"How?" asked the boy.

"Each of us was a wealthy merchant, such as you are,"

1 Tiflis refers to Tbilisi, the capital of Georgia.

said the men; "we went to Tiflis and there heard that the King had a daughter called the World's Beauty. We wished to see her, and they charged each of us forty pieces of gold to behold her from behind a glass partition. We fell in love with her, and thereafter spent all our wealth to see her over and over again. So we wasted eighty camel-loads of merchandise and to-day we are so poor that no one cares to look at us."

The boy gave them a handful of gold coins, and on the next day loaded his camels and started for Tiflis. He gave forty gold coins to see the World's Beauty from behind the glass, and after that spent all his wealth and merchandise for her sake. He came back to Bagdad to his mother, as poor as Job, and told her his ill-luck. She scolded him for his disobedience to his father's command. But the boy wept and promised that he would not go to Tiflis any more, if she gave him from his father's secret chamber something by which he could earn his living and preserve his father's reputation. His mother gave him an empty purse, saying:

"If to-day you put in this purse forty pieces of copper, on the morrow you will see that they have changed to forty pieces of gold. After three years, the gold put into the purse changes into copper. That is to say, once in three years the talisman changes to its contrary."

"This is good," thought the boy; "I have now an inexhaustible revenue, which never requires work."

He soon forgot his promise to his mother, and took the first caravan

to go to Tiflis. He paid forty gold pieces every day to see the World's Beauty, and his money was not exhausted. The maiden was surprised, and one day invited him to a banquet, with the intention of robbing him.

"Ah! I love you very much," she said to him, artfully,

"I will certainly marry you if you tell me the secret of your wealth."

How easily may a simple youth be deceived by an artful woman! The boy fell into the trap and showed her the magic purse. The maiden intoxicated him with poisonous wine, and taking away the purse expelled him from her house. He returned to his mother, lamenting his loss. He wept and promised not to go again to Tiflis, if she gave him something else from his father's secret chamber by which he might earn his living. A mother's heart is tender; she could not resist his importunities, and at last brought to him from the secret chamber a cap, saying:

"This is a magic cap; when you put it on your head you will see others without being seen by anybody."

This was something that suited the boy best of all. As soon as he became the owner of the cap he forgot his solemn promises to his mother and directly set out for the city of Tiflis. He entered the maiden's house and looked at her as much as he pleased, without being molested. The maiden and the inmates of the house detected that there was somebody in the house, but they could not see him, despite their repeated efforts. One day, the maiden thought it might be the youth of Bagdad who was playing this trick, and she called him by his name, saying:

"Disclose yourself, I will certainly marry you."

The boy took the cap from his head, and appeared to the maiden.

"O, my dear lord," said the wily maiden, "I have been burning for your love. Ever since you have gone away I have uttered no name but yours, and I am yours still if you tell me your secret."

The boy was deceived by her artful words and told her

the secret of the cap. A banquet was given to the boy, poisonous wine was served to him, and the cap being taken from him he was expelled from the house, with disgrace. He came back to Bagdad, begging his way. He had no heart to go again to his mother. He entreated the intervention of friends and kinsfolk, who persuaded the mother and reconciled her with her prodigal son. He begged his mother for a third secret from his father's chamber.

"But one secret is left," she said. "If you lose this one also, we shall become hungry and naked, and become paupers."

She gave the boy a horn, and told him to blow it. The boy blew it, and lo! the mountains and plains were covered with soldiers.

"Now," she said, "blow it from the other end."

He did so, and lo! the army disappeared.

"Mamma," said the boy, "now let me go, fight with my enemies and

bring back all that I have lost."

Thus speaking he set out without waiting for an answer. As soon as he arrived at Tiflis, he stood upon the hilltop near the city and blew the horn. In the twinkling of an eye the city was besieged by an army so great that there was no room left for the soldiers to stand on. There was a sudden panic in the city; all the people were terrified. The King sent messengers to the boy, asking him what he wanted.

"War! War!" exclaimed the boy. "Who do you think I am?"

They recognized him and saw that he was the boy of Bagdad. Thereupon the King called his daughter, saying:

"You are the cause of this trouble; go see the boy and quench this fire, before we both perish."

The maiden sent a messenger to the boy, saying:

"I will come to you, my love, and we will go directly to the church to be married, and then go to our house. But, love, disperse your army that I may come to you."

Soon after the message the maiden herself appeared. The boy blew the horn from the other end, and the army disappeared. The maiden coming to the boy, apologized for the past and poured out all her store of sweet and fascinating words. She brought also a letter from her father approving of their marriage. The boy told the maiden the secret of the horn, but this time did not give it to her.

"Well, then," said the maiden, "put the horn in your trunk, lock and seal it, and let us send it home. One cannot go to church with a horn in one's pocket; it is a sin. After the wedding we will return home, examine the seal of the trunk, and open it. Nobody will steal your horn."

The boy consented, and putting the horn in the box, sealed it and sent it to the maiden's house. When they reached the church door, the maiden suddenly exclaimed:

"O me! I forgot to kiss the hand of my father and mother. Let me go and bid them farewell, then I will come and the wedding will take place."

The boy believed her and let her go. Coming to the house, she ordered her servants to break the trunk. She got out the horn, sent a man to the boy and expelled him with disgrace from the city. The boy was now at a complete loss. He had no more hope in his mother, and no favor in the sight of his countrymen. For a time he wandered here and there and then decided to go to sea.

"Let me go," he thought, "to the end of the world, to an unknown country, where nobody will know me."

He was accepted as a servant on board a ship. But soon after they sailed there was a heavy storm on the sea, and the ship was wrecked. The boy was saved on a piece of board, and was cast upon an uninhabited island where he lived eating wild berries. One day he saw two apple-trees growing near one another; the fruit of one was of common size, but the fruit of the other tree was as large as a man's head, and very tempting to eat.

"What a nice fruit!" thought the boy, and ate one of the large apples. As soon as he tasted it, lo! he became a donkey, with a tail and very long ears. As a four-legged beast, for a time he grazed in the neighborhood; only he was conscious that he was a man and had become a donkey. One day, as he was grazing near the two apple-trees, he ate one of the small apples which had fallen down from the tree, and lo! he became a man as before.

"This is well," thought the boy, "I can make good use of these wonderful fruits."

He picked up a good many of the apples of both kinds. One day he saw a ship sailing at a distance. He displayed a signal and the ship sailed to the island. He went on board, taking both kinds of apples with him. The sailors pitied him and brought him back to Tiflis without charge. The boy disguised himself, and taking the shape of a peddler, went to the neighborhood of the house of the King's daughter, to sell his large apples. The maiden was greatly pleased with the appearance of the fruit, and paying twenty pieces of gold, bought two large apples. She and her forty maids ate slices of the apples, and all of them were suddenly changed into donkeys, and went out into the yard braying. It is said that as a donkey also the World's Beauty was excellent. The King came with his peers who, seeing what had happened, were greatly surprised and grieved. By this time the boy was again disguised, taking the shape of a doctor, and calling himself Dr. Karabobo. The

King's servants summoned all the doctors of the city, but it was of no avail. At last they said to the King that there was left only a certain Dr. Karabobo, a foreigner.

"Bring him hither," said the King.

By that time all the followers of secret arts crowded about the King's palace. Priests, monks, astrologers, star-gazers, magicians, sorcerers, witches, wizards, necromancers, bird conjurers, mice conjurers, snake conjurers, predictors by measuring with the span, predictors by casting beans or blue pebbles, predictors by gazing at cups of water, and all kinds of enchanters, male and female, old and young, were there, practicing their arts, but none could understand the secret, or devise a remedy. They all, however, were unanimous in declaring that it was a punishment sent from heaven to chastise the World's Beauty for her arbitrary cruelties. Thereupon Dr. Karabobo came in and said to the King:

"I can transform these donkeys once more into human beings, but only on two conditions; first, that you give to me your daughter in marriage, and secondly, that you also give me whatever I desire."

"I agree to do so," answered the King.

The agreement was written, signed and sealed by the King and his twelve peers. The boy took the document, and putting it in his pocket, said:

"First of all, I want you to bring hither the eighty camel-loads of merchandise, which your daughter stole from two merchants."

The King gave orders and they were brought.

"Now bring," he added, "the forty loads which were taken from the youth of Bagdad; bring his magic purse, cap, and horn, and also the gold coins which were, during the past years, taken from the magic purse at the rate of forty gold pieces a day."

The King and his lords were surprised that he knew all this, but were obliged to bring what he asked, according to the agreement. The King only begged him not to demand the gold which the purse had held, as there was not enough in the royal treasury to make up so large a sum. But Dr. Karabobo was inflexible; he held the horn in readiness to call the army, if needed. Then he drew the small apples out of his pocket and gave a piece to every donkey, whereupon they were transformed into human beings. After that he told them who he was. He took the maiden and all belonging to him and set out for Bagdad. He blew the horn and an immense army accompanied him. Thus with a princely procession he came to the city of Erzerum, where he found the two ex-merchants and restored to them their property. Then he entered Bagdad with great pomp, and said to his mother, who had gone to meet him:

"Mother, here are all my possessions, and here is the maiden who tortured your son so much. I was obliged to become an ass before I learned how to treat her, and it was necessary for her to become an ass before she ceased to be a deceitful shrew. She is now a human being and promises to become a submissive daughter-in-law."

The maiden then kissed both hands of the aged woman as a token of her obedience. They celebrated their wedding festival for forty days, after which they went to the church and were married.

SALMAN AND ROSTOM

Salman was a strong and mighty man, He was as large as a hill, as powerful as a giant, and a terrible tyrant. He lived in one corner of the world, but his fame spread terror over all the earth. He had a horse of lightning, and his arms were as strong as iron. He assaulted men in their peaceful habitations, and took tribute from them; none could refuse to pay him tribute, else he would slaughter and destroy the people. In another portion of the earth there was another strong brigand, called Chal, who had a son named Rostom. This Rostom was a huge man, as large as a mountain, and greatly celebrated for his extraordinary strength and bravery. It was only the land of this Chal which did not pay tribute to Salman.

One day Chal mounted his horse and started, saying: "Let me go and see what kind of a man Salman is."

After a long journey he met a huge man mounted on a horse swift as lightning; the staff of his spear was as thick as a man's waist. Chal did not know that this was Salman himself; but nevertheless he prepared his spear for battle. To his surprise, the horseman gave spur to his horse and passed by Chal without even looking at his face. Upon this Chal was offended, and threw his spear after the horseman. Salman turned back, seized Chal, whom he bound under the belly of his horse, and galloped until he came to a tent pitched by a gurgling spring. He dismounted, nailed Chal's ear to the tent's beam, and lay down to sleep. Chal was almost mad with rage; he gnashed his teeth and muttered to himself:

"He did not speak a word to me, he did not tell me his name. I wish I might know who he is."

Salman soon waked, and asked:

"Fellow, who are you?"

"I am from Chal's country," answered Chal. He was so much afraid that he did not say that he was Chal himself.

"Ah!" exclaimed Salman, releasing Chal's ear, "why did you not tell me before? Go and bid Rostom, Chal's son, come hither that we may measure swords. There cannot be two men of equal strength; the world must know who is the stronger champion. I am Salman."

Chal returned to his house and sighed deeply. Rostom, hearing him sighing, said:

"How now, father? You are Chal and I am Rostom, your son, and yet you sigh! Nay, you must tell me your grief."

Chal told him of his meeting with Salman, and the latter's challenge to Rostom. Rostom took with him his cousin Vyjhan, and both disguised themselves, assuming the habit of pilgrims. Rostom kissed his white-hoofed horse on both eyes and said to his father:

"When I am in trouble my horse will know it and will beat the ground with his feet. Then bind my arms upon his back and set him free; he will come and find me."

Vyjhan, who accompanied Rostom on his journey, was far from being a common mortal. He had a wonderful voice; if he cried in the East his voice would be heard in the West. After traveling for a long time, Rostom and Vyjhan came to a city and encamped upon a meadow outside the town. Rostom was sleeping, when Vyjhan heard a terrible uproar in the city and went there to inquire the cause of the trouble. Some of the people were running like chased deer, some were tearing their hair, some beating their breasts, and all were weeping and wailing.

"Why, what is the matter?" asked Vyjhan.

"Salman has come, demanding seven years' tribute that is in arrears," the people answered.

Soon they collected the amount; but the question now arose, by whom they should send the tribute, because Salman would take away the man by whom the tribute was sent, and kill him.

"Give it to me, I will take it," said Vyjhan.

Soon Rostom heard in his sleep Vyjhan's shrill voice, saying:

"Help, Rostom! Salman is carrying me away."

Rostom got up and learned from the people what had happened, and lo! his white-hoofed horse came running and stood before him. Immediately Rostom jumped on the back of his horse, which galloped away and soon reached Salman's tent. Salman, having nailed Vyjhan's ear to the tent beam, came out to meet Rostom. Then and there took place a duel the most terrible that has ever been recorded in the history of the world. Bows and arrows, spears and swords were cut into pieces. Finally they came near one another, seized each other, and both were entangled in each other's hair.

Up to the present time they have not yet conquered one another, but are still struggling. Now and then they pull and shake each other so violently that the earth quakes, and that is what men call an earthquake; and Vyjhan's voice is still heard deeply from afar.

THE SPARROW AND THE TWO CHILDREN

Vart was the name of a boy who was six years old, and Vartoohi was the name of his sister, who was five years of age. Varteni, their dear mother, had died, and Vartan, their father, had brought home a stepmother who had with her a boy of her own four years old. Vartan was a well-to-do farmer, and as he loved his children he brought them nice suits of clothes and dresses, delicious food, pretty toys and many other presents. The stepmother, being a wicked woman, envied the little half-orphans and wished to destroy them that she might secure every good thing for her own child. In order to attain her vile purpose she secretly boiled the seed that her husband was to sow in the field that year. The wheat, of course, did not grow, and as there was no crop, the farmer had to borrow to meet his expenses. The following year she played the same treacherous trick and increased the farmer's indebtedness so much that the poor man, giving up every hope of the farm, went away to sojourn in other countries to earn money. That was what the wicked woman desired with all her heart. She fed her son with meat and pies, while she gave the half-orphans only a handful of boiled wheat to eat. One day she decided to take Vart and Vartoohi to the river as if to bathe them, and there to drown them. That day the two innocent half-orphans had taken their handful of boiled wheat and were eating it in a corner of the yard. They saw a small sparrow that was jumping and hopping around them, and chirping and chattering as it leaped. Vart wanted to kill it with a stone, but Vartoohi prevented him. As they were eating their poor, scanty meal, they listened to the little birdie, and lo! they thought they could understand what it was chirping.

"Orphans, orphans! good little orphans!" the little sparrow was saying, "give me a few grains which I may take to my little ones in my tiny nest and I will give you good counsel."

The children cast a few grains to the bird, which after taking them to its nest came back, saying:

"Orphans, run! orphans, run! your stepmother will to-day take you to the river to drown you. Run, orphans, run!"

And the little sparrow flew away. Soon the stepmother came, saying:

"Get up, you dirty things! we will go to the river, where I may bathe you."

"You go first, mamma; we will come by and by," answered the orphans.

And following the advice of their little feathered friend they ran away to the mountains. The stepmother never searched for them, and the two children wandered in the forest until evening. At nightfall they entered the hollow trunk of an old sycamore tree, repeated the prayer which they had learned from their dead mother, and lay down to sleep embracing one another. Soon after daybreak the faithful sparrow came, and the two children waking heard it chirp to them:

"Orphans, good orphans, come and eat; there is boiled wheat for you."

They immediately got up and ran after the sparrow, which led them until they came where an old woman brought a kettleful of boiled wheat, and emptying it under a tree, went away. A great many little sparrows were gathered; the two half-orphans sat with them at the table. The good old woman used to bring the kettleful of wheat and empty it under that tree day after day. She did this in memory of her children and grandchildren, who had died when they were young boys and girls, and whom she had loved very much. She believed that these little birdies were the spirits of her dead little ones. So these two half-orphans lived with the little sparrows for a long time.

One day as the Prince was hunting in the forest he met Vart and Vartoohi, took them with him to the palace, loved them and adopted them as his son and daughter. The children were so pretty and amiable that all the court loved them dearly. But Vart and Vartoohi were not happy.

"What is the matter with you, my children?" asked the Prince; "what is the cause of your grief?"

"We long to see our dear papa who has gone away," answered Vart.

"And we long to see the little sparrow, our benefactor," added Vartoohi.

The Prince sent out men in search of Vartan, the father of the children; and finding him, brought him home. He punished his wife for her wickedness, and embraced his children. The Prince kept him also, as a messenger in the court. But who could find the sparrow? It came by itself one day, and alighting on the window where the orphans were, chirped:

"You blessed little orphans, you pitied my little ones and gave me grain, and lo! Heaven has bestowed upon you so many bounties. May you continue to be blessed and to be happy."

The Prince liked the little sparrow for its good services and permitted it to build its nest thereafter under the eaves of the palace. All sparrows which at the present time build their nests under the eaves of houses are the descendants of that good sparrow. Let us be good even to the sparrows and they may bring good to us.

SOPHENE